Scottish Relic Trilogy Box Set

Love and Mayhem

The Promise (Pennington Family)

The Rebel

Secret Vows Box Set

Borrowed Dreams (Scottish Dream Trilogy Book 1)

Captured Dreams (Book 2)

Dreams of Destiny (Book 3)

Scottish Dream Trilogy Box Set

Romancing the Scot

Sweet Home Highland Christmas

It Happened in the Highlands

Sleepless in Scotland

Dearest Millie

How to Ditch a Duke

A Prince in the Pantry

Jane Austen Cannot Marry!

Highland Crown (Royal Highlander Series Book 1)

Highland Jewel (Book 2)

Highland Sword (Book 3)

Ghost of the Thames

Thanksgiving in Connecticut

Made in Heaven

Marriage of Minds: Collaborative Writing *(Nonfiction)*

Step Write Up: Writing Exercises for 21st Century *(Nonfiction)*

Aquarian

Omid's Shadow

SWEET HOME HIGHLAND CHRISTMAS

A Pennington Novella

MAY MCGOLDRICK

Book Duo Creative

Thank you for choosing *Sweet Home Highland Christmas*. In the event that you appreciate this book, please consider sharing the good word(s) by leaving a review, or connect with the authors.

Cover by Dar Albert, WickedSmartDesigns.com

❧　I　❧

Sutherland
The Scottish Highlands
December 11, 1817

CAPTAIN GREGORY PENNINGTON put down the knife and fork and glanced around at the crowded coffee room. Where were these blasted people he was to escort to Baronsford?

With only a fortnight till Christmas, he had every right to be impatient. The ice and wind had made the trip down the coast road to Helmsdale difficult, and the rest of the journey south to the Borders didn't promise to be any better. They'd need most of those days to reach the family estate, and he was anxious to get there.

The room buzzed with voices and activity. Thick clouds of tobacco hung beneath the blackened rafters, and the warm damp smell of wet wool and salty sea air filled his senses. Travelers from a northbound coach were huddled by the roaring fire, stamping their feet and warming themselves, and every table was filled. It appeared that everyone on the east coast of Scotland was trying to get home.

Home. Penn thought about the changes at Baronsford. Of anywhere in the world, the old castle was always home. He and his brother and three sisters had spent every summer there on the River Tweed—running through the forests, riding, swimming, and sunning themselves on the rock in the lake. It had been a splendid place to grow up.

Change was an inevitable factor in life. He knew that, and Baronsford had undergone change, to be sure. After the deaths of his brother Hugh's first wife and son, an eight-year chill had descended over the place.

But, as winter eventually turns to spring, life had finally returned to Baronsford. His brother and his new wife were making it a home again. Penn had seen it when he attended their wedding this past June. It was a happy change. The house once again glowed with warmth and sunshine. And now Grace was with child. Another generation of Penningtons was about to begin.

Penn's thoughts lingered on his family. Every Christmas, they all went home to the Borders. Regardless of the clergy's position on Yule celebrations, Baronsford hosted one of its two annual balls the day after Christmas. So many members of the realm's leading families braved northern England's and Scotland's often fierce winter weather to attend the event. And every year, along with the festivities, Penn faced the inevitable teasing from his mother and sisters about marriage.

He still held the opinion that he'd never marry until he put down solid roots in a place of his own. As the second son of an earl, he'd thrown himself into forging a life. A builder by nature, a commission with the Royal Engineers had provided him with a career he needed. Until now.

Lately, he'd grown discontented with military life, with the lack of permanence—both in location and in relationships. He was increasingly conscious of how tired he was of being unable to plan his own life with the same precision that he built roads or bridges. And with the wars with France finally over, the government was focusing on its colonies abroad. There was a great deal to do in India and Canada and Australia, but he wanted no part in that. Not any longer.

Penn had already given his notice to the Corps of his plan to relinquish his commission. He needed a new adventure. A new life. He was ready to look for a place to settle down and build a home and perhaps practice the profession that he still loved. Then, he'd entertain the idea of marriage.

The destination he had in mind would be certain to cause a stir with his family. Boston in America. A growing city that was, by all accounts, bursting at the seams. Though he'd never been there himself, the Penningtons were no strangers to the place. His uncle and wife and his cousins lived there, so Penn had connections. Still, it was far away.

He planned on announcing the news of the move to the family this Christmas.

Penn looked around the coffee room. So where were these people? If he'd ridden south as he planned, he'd be halfway to Baronsford by now. But his brother's letter—along with a carriage—had reached him the day before he was to leave. It was a curious note. As Lord Justice, Hugh was painstakingly explicit, but the message had been uncharacteristically cryptic. Penn was to connect up with four adults and a child in Helmsdale. They were traveling from an estate in Sutherland to the Borders to meet with Lady Dacre, a neighbor of his parents in Hertfordshire.

A door opened and a gust of wind carried a coachman inside.

"*Ceathrú uaire*! Fifteen minutes afore departure north!" the man shouted, clapping his wool-clad hands and glaring about him. "Be in yer places or be left!"

A barmaid pushed by Penn, carrying food to a young couple sitting with their hands entwined at a table in the corner. Newlyweds, he thought, wondering where home was for them.

Penn's eyes roamed from table to table, searching for the people he was to convey to Baronsford. A few travelers were moving toward the door, wrapping their mufflers and coats around them in preparation for the next stage of their journey.

The sensation of being watched drew Penn's gaze around the room again until he saw, standing right at his elbow, a child bundled in a mulberry-colored greatcoat. Inside the fur-trimmed hood, light brown curls framed a small, rosy-cheeked face. Little as she was, the girl lit the grey room with color. Alert, slanted brown eyes, dark as night, stared intently at him. She didn't wait for him to speak.

"How old are you?" the cherub asked gravely.

Penn looked around for the child's family. There was little chance of a lass getting lost in a place like this, but he was relieved to see a wafer-thin woman keeping an eye on his visitor from a nearby table.

"Thirty." Penn pushed his plate away. "And you?"

"Do you have children?" she continued, ignoring his

question.

The woman watching them began to rise just as the barmaid delivered plates of food to their table.

"None," he replied. "That I know of."

An eyebrow cocked slightly. "Any wife...that you know of?"

Penn wondered if he'd been mistaken in thinking this tiny female was a child. Though she appeared to be no more than five or six, she seemed to understand more than she should for her age.

"No wives," he told her. "*That* I'm sure of."

"Are you a pauper, then?"

"A pauper?" Penn repeated, trying not to smile. Echoes of similar conversations he'd had with his sisters rang in his ears.

"It's a simple question."

"No, I'm not a pauper."

"Then why haven't you married? You're old enough. You wear a uniform. You're not a pauper."

"Has my father sent you?" he asked. "Or was it my mother?"

She stepped a little closer and curled her finger at him. Penn leaned down as she lowered her voice and asked in a confidential tone, "You're not a papist, are you?"

Penn shook his head, afraid he'd laugh if he tried to reply and sensing that his interrogator might have been offended at such a response.

"*Giùlain thu fhèin*, Ella. Behave yourself," the woman said, coming up to the table. "I'm sorry that she's bothering you, Captain. This wee miss can be a bit troublesome, I fear."

"Not at all," he replied.

"This is my nursemaid," Ella told him.

"I see." Penn nodded politely.

"Come, lassie. You've a hot plate of stew waiting for you at our table." The woman tried to take the child's hand, but Ella squirmed out of reach.

"May I have just ten minutes to converse with this gentleman?"

"Nay. It's time to eat."

"Five then?"

"Ella..."

"Two minutes. He said I'm not bothering him. Please, Shona," the young girl drawled with the practiced skill of an actress who knew how to win her audience. "Two. Only two. I have something to say to him. Please."

The maid's exasperated expression told Penn that this was a regular episode. She shook her head.

"Give me one minute, and I promise I'll finish my dinner and sit quietly until the next stop."

"We both know there's about as good a chance of that happening as..." Shona looked apologetically at Penn. "If you're certain she's not bothering you, Captain. I'm right there. Please just send her on her way if she gets to be too much."

Penn was entertained. His lifestyle excluded any regular interaction with children. What he knew of them was through the stories his men shared. The infants didn't sleep. As soon as they could walk, they were prone to bumps and bruises and were constantly underfoot. Five- and six-year-olds? He didn't know what that age was like, but whatever his impression might have been, this child didn't fit it.

Ella waited until the nursemaid sat at the adjoining table before she spoke.

"Shona is married to Dougal. He's outside now,

looking after our luggage. They married three years ago." She held out three fingers. "The reason why they don't have children is because I fixed them."

"Fixed them?" he asked, giving up trying to hide his smile.

"A wee bit troublesome?" She shook her head gravely. "I am a *lot* troublesome."

And amusing. Penn wondered what the parents of this little one were like. The child's intelligence and independent spirit had to be a challenge. He recalled his brother's letter. He was to accompany four adults and a child to Baronsford. He wondered if this was the child.

"Where are you traveling to from here, Miss Ella?" he asked.

"I don't think it would be quite proper for me to answer, do you?" She didn't wait for his answer and shrugged. "Fie says we must be on our best behavior during this journey. Grandfather told her that's not bloody likely."

"Your grandfather said that, did he?"

The curly head bobbed once.

"Perhaps if I introduced myself, we could converse more properly," he said. "My name is Captain Gregory Pennington, but to my friends, I'm just Penn."

"Well, I'm Ella, which is what everyone calls me. Except for Grandfather. He has a number of names for me that Fie says I mustn't repeat."

Remembering that she needed to curtsy, she did so. And as a smile pulled at her lips, two dimples formed in her cheeks.

Before he could respond, the door to the coach yard opened and a taller, older version of his miniature inquisitor sailed into the coffee room. Brown eyes that matched Ella's swept the crowd and the hood fell back, giving Penn a clear view of the red-cheeked beauty. He had no doubt to whom the little girl belonged.

Cloaked in a blue greatcoat, the woman paused inside the door and pulled gloves from her hands as she looked for her party. From the balanced stance to the set of her jaw, everything about her indicated strength and confidence, and only served to enhance her beauty. A high forehead and clear eyes dominated her perfectly symmetrical features. The full pursed lips stirred something in him that he preferred not to be entertaining, considering the circumstances.

Aware that Penn's attention had been diverted, Ella turned and saw the woman by the door.

"That's Fie," she told him, running between tables toward her.

"Fie" lifted the child as small arms wrapped around her neck. The two presented a mirror image. A quick kiss, and then matching dimples formed in their cheeks as they looked into each other's eyes. The woman whispered a few words to Ella and pressed a kiss on her forehead. The little one planted a return kiss on her forehead. Kisses were required on each cheek and returned in kind. Penn recognized a ritual when he saw one. They made a beautiful pair, and he realized others were staring at the two, as well.

As he watched her put the child down, Penn waited to see the lucky bastard who was due to follow Fie in from the yard. No one came in. So where was the husband? The two came hand in hand to the table where the nursemaid waited.

Penn couldn't help himself. His attention was riveted to their table.

"*Cá bhfuil sé?*" the nursemaid asked in Gaelic. "The colonel isn't here?" the nursemaid asked.

There was a slight shake of the head as the younger woman tried to encourage Ella to sit at the table.

"What'll you do, mistress?"

Fie sent another silent plea to the nursemaid to divert the conversation, but it appeared to be too late.

"He's not here?" Ella blurted out, looking up.

"No, my love," Fie responded. "But don't worry. We have to make many stops along the way. He has ample opportunity to catch up to us."

"But that won't do," Ella said, raising her voice and scrambling off the bench.

"Don't worry yourself, sweetheart. Why don't you—"

"No, Fie. No. We have a great deal to worry about." She glanced at Penn and tugged on the mother's arm. "But I can fix this. Come. Come with me."

He watched as the young girl tried to turn the adult toward his table.

"He's thirty years old, not married, and not a pauper. And I like him better than Colonel Richard."

The woman leaned over the child. "Honey, you have no reason to fret. We'll be—"

"No, Fie! Listen to me!" Stamping her foot, she pointed at Penn. "You have to ask *him* to marry you. Please. Then you can keep me."

———

Then you can keep me.

The sudden shock of embarrassment before this stranger was immediately replaced by the clawing pain she felt at Ella's unhappy outburst. Freya Sutherland had made every effort to shield her niece from the potential outcome of this trip, but the lassie saw and heard everything. She was everywhere. And she was a five-year-old going on twenty-five.

For over a month now, the Sutherland household had been in an uproar regarding the Dowager Lady Dacre's request and how it would affect all of their futures. She realized now it was foolish to think the anxiety they were feeling would go unnoticed by the child.

Freya crouched down until she was at eye level with Ella and placed the tip of her finger on the girl's trembling chin. Brown eyes met hers, and Ella reached out, replicating the gesture. Freya hadn't realized that she herself was on the verge of losing control.

Neither of them was prone to shedding tears. They were aunt and niece, but they could as well have been mother and daughter. Ella was only a week old when Freya's sister, Lucy, died of complications after childbirth. The infant's father was off fighting Napoleon on the battlefields of Spain. On her deathbed, Lucy had entrusted her bairn to her sister, and Fredrick Dacre was more than amenable to the arrangement, having been cut off by his family at the time of his marriage. It still bothered Freya that he'd never lived to see his daughter.

For five years, the Sutherlands had lived in peace, thinking the final letter from the father was enough to assign the guardianship of Ella to them permanently. But now, everything was about to change, one way or another. Fredrick's mother, the widow of the late Duke of St. Albans, was insisting on the assurance that her granddaughter's future was secure with Freya and "those Scotch people." Courts sided with wealth, so Ella's future needed to be decided through diplomacy and not legal battles.

"You won't let me go, Fie, will you?" the child asked.

"Never," Freya whispered, pulling Ella tightly into her arms.

"But you need to marry to keep me."

"I'll marry," Freya whispered against the soft curls. "You're staying with me."

"But Colonel Richard isn't here. He was supposed to meet us, wasn't he?"

"He'll join us in Dundee," Freya lied, hoping the weather and the condition of the roads were the cause of Dunbar's delay. "The colonel is very excited that I've finally accepted his offer. He'll join us, and I'll marry when the time comes."

Ella pulled out of her arms. "But you don't like him."

"Of course I like him," Freya lied again, upset that her feelings were so transparent.

She *had* to marry. There was no other way. Even though her father, Sutherland of Torrishbrae, was in perfect health, he was getting older. With no son, the estate she'd spent her entire life on was destined to go to a distant cousin, Colonel Richard Dunbar, a conceited, arrogant, military commander. Everyone in Scotland knew that the colonel's interest in Freya lay mainly with her own fortune, and she'd been putting off responding to his offer of marriage for years. But now, with the dowager's stipulation that Ella must have a permanent and stable home, as well as secure provisions for the future, Freya had no choice.

"I like him well enough," she said again, trying to sound more definite.

"You're being a bloody martyr," Ella said.

"What did I tell you about using your grandfather's bad language?" Freya scolded, pushing to her feet.

"You said I had to stop talking like Grandfather *when* we get to Baronsford."

In the periphery of her vision, she saw the red-coated officer at the next table stand and approach.

"I meant now, forever. You very well know you need to act your age."

"Only if *you* act your age."

Freya frowned at her own expression mirrored in the little face. The tall gentleman stood over them. She cringed at the thought of what he must think, having heard their conversation. She took Ella's hand firmly in her own and sent her a warning glare before turning to him.

The man's broad, scarlet-coated chest nearly blocked her view of the rest of the dining room. Her eyes focused momentarily on gold lace, the blue facing, and the glinting epaulets.

"My sincere apologies, Captain, for intruding on you."

She was suddenly caught up in the most beautiful eyes she'd ever seen on a man. They were a deep shade of blue and were fringed with long dark lashes.

"I...we shouldn't...we didn't mean to..."

"Fie never stammers," Ella said matter-of-factly to the tall stranger. "She's embarrassed."

"I am *not* embarrassed," Freya said to her niece. "I'm apologizing."

"Then do it," the rascal said. "We're listening."

Who was the adult here? she thought. Freya turned her attention back to the gentleman who continued to stand there, the hint of a smirk on his face. He was handsome in a way that unsettled her. Dark brown hair curled neatly around his ears. The strong square chin and chiseled cheekbones made her want to pause and appreciate the perfect arrangement of his face. The small scar above his eyebrow did nothing to lessen his handsome looks. He was a man from one of Mrs. Radcliffe's novels come to life, a man whom a woman dreamt of and never imagined meeting.

"Please forgive our rather forward disposition. If you'd be kind enough to return to your—"

"The gentleman is finished with his dinner, Fie," Ella whispered loudly. "He's waiting for an introduction."

A smile pulled at the man's lips. "The young lady is correct. I am, if you'd not be offended by *my* forwardness."

Freya's mouth went dry. Whatever objection she was about to voice deserted her at once. Her lack of social interaction—outside of their small country circle—was no excuse for her foolish response to the gentleman, though it was true that their life in the Highlands had limited her acquaintance with such men.

"I think he's far more suitable than Colonel Richard."

Ella's loud whisper had to be heard by everyone in the coffee room.

"That will do," Freya said firmly.

The little imp shrugged and then looked at the captain.

"May I present Miss Freya Sutherland," Ella announced.

His surprised look moved from Freya's face to her niece and back. She could perfectly understand the confusion. Ella understood it, as well.

"I'm an orphan. Fie is my aunt and my guardian," the girl explained. "Grandfather also looks after me, but he threatens to use me as fish bait when I'm behaving like an eldritch creature."

Despite her mortification, Freya had to stifle a laugh. She could hear her father saying exactly those words.

Without a pause, Ella continued her introduction "And this is Captain Penny...Penny..."

"Pennington," he contributed with a bow.

Freya curtsied, but she knew the name. The Dowager Lady Dacre's letter had mentioned that her friends, the Pennington family, would make the arrangements for their transportation to the Borders. Her gaze fixed on the stranger.

"You're the person we're to travel with."

"That's brilliant," Ella announced, smiling.

"I hope your trip here was uneventful." His gaze moved to the table behind her. "I was informed that I would be accompanying four adults and a child."

"At the moment, we are a party of three adults and a child," Freya corrected. "Ella's nurse, a manservant, and the two of us. I'm afraid my cousin...my intended...has been unexpectedly detained. I'm certain he'll catch up to us at one of our stops."

"But maybe he won't," Ella added, leaning against her aunt's legs while eyeing the captain.

The little girl had a habit of speaking what was on Freya's mind, but it wasn't quite so cute here in the presence of this stranger.

"Where is he coming from?"

"Fort William. Perhaps he'll meet us at Inverness."

"You said Dundee," Ella chirped.

"What is your cousin's name?" the captain asked.

Freya hesitated for a moment as she tried to decide on how much she wanted to disclose to their escort. As a Pennington, he was a friend of the Dacres. In her exchange of letters with the dowager, she'd informed the woman that she'd be bringing her fiancé, even though the understanding with her cousin wasn't exactly official.

"Colonel Richard Dunbar," she said.

The forehead furrowed as something registered.

"Do you know him?" Freya asked.

"I know of him." The man glanced away.

As Ella took Freya's hand, the words they both uttered were exactly the same. "Is something wrong?"

His gaze rested on Ella for a moment before coming back to Freya's face. He shook his head. Something *was* wrong, but Captain Pennington was not about to discuss it before the child.

"Privacy, sweetheart."

Ella stamped her foot once, but then wordlessly retreated to her nursemaid. Some people thought Freya was too lenient with her niece, but it wasn't true. When it mattered, when it was time, Ella understood and reacted appropriately to her aunt's wishes.

Freya moved in the direction of the fireplace and their escort followed. "What is it, Captain?"

"You have an understanding with Colonel Dunbar?"

She did, but she didn't. Freya didn't know how much of her situation she cared to explain. "Why do you ask, sir?"

"The officers here in the Highlands are a fairly close-knit group, Miss Sutherland."

He hesitated, clearly weighing his words.

"And?"

"Word has been circulating for a fortnight or more that Colonel Dunbar is to be married to an heiress, a Miss Katherine Caithness. The wedding was to take place today."

2

THERE HAD TO BE A MISTAKE. Her cousin wouldn't abandon her at the last minute.

As the carriage rolled along the frozen road, gusts of wind buffeted the sides of the vehicle. Freya thought back. His last letter had been addressed to her less than a fortnight ago. He said he was *eager* to accompany her to Baronsford for the Christmas Ball. Meeting Lady Dacre would be an honor, he wrote. He was *delighted* that Freya had finally come to her senses regarding his offer of marriage.

Freya was certain he understood what was at stake.

She wouldn't lose Ella. Giving her niece over to the Dacre family was not an option. Freya's late brother-in-law had twelve brothers and sisters, and not one of them had reached out to her sister when she was alive. And in the five years since Lucy's death, not one of them had shown any interest in even meeting Ella.

It was only in the wake of her husband's death that Lady Dacre felt any remorse over ignoring her granddaughter. Suddenly, she was filled with concern about Ella's future. She said proof was needed that the Sutherlands of Torrishbrae were fit to care for a member of *her* family. And in referring to the Sutherlands, she meant Freya, who'd taken responsibility for Ella from that first dark day.

Back at the inn, when Captain Pennington told her the rumor about her cousin, Freya had asserted that he was misinformed. What he'd heard must have been a mistake. She desperately hoped she was correct.

Emotions clawed at her heart before knotting into a fist in her throat. Freya clenched her jaw and focused on the wintry countryside outside of the carriage window. The ice-covered tops of Craig Riasgain and Beinn Mhealaich stood silent and formidable against the steel blue sky and the encroaching clouds. She had to stay strong. Never give up. It was up to her to secure her niece's future. Ella belonged with her.

Despite the icy ruts and dips in the road that jarred them occasionally, they were moving steadily southward. Her manservant, Dougal, was riding up top with the captain's men. She was relieved that her niece at least for now had abandoned the idea of a marriage of convenience between the captain and Freya. Exhaustion had claimed the five-year-old and, sometime after setting out, Ella had put her head down in Freya's lap and gone to sleep. Shona, bundled in a blanket across from her, was blessed with a similar ability to ignore the discomforts of travel. Freya watched the maid unconsciously wedge her head into the corner of the carriage, and it wasn't long before a soft snore escaped her.

Freya's gaze shifted to the man sitting next to Shona. With Ella curled up on the seat, Captain Pennington had plenty of room for his long, muscular legs. He'd stored his sword and black bicorne hat in a compartment beneath the seat, where she saw a brace of pistols. As he looked out the window, her eyes lingered on his strong hands. She knew little about his character, except that the dowager had entrusted their care to him. Whatever Freya thought of Lady Dacre, that spoke highly of the captain.

Her gaze drifted upward over his grey kersey greatcoat to his handsome face. His head rested against the back wall of the carriage. She stared at the cleft in his chin and sensual lips, and for an insane moment, her thoughts flickered back to that time years ago when she'd dreamed of attending her first season and her first ball. Her imaginings had never been about a full dance card or a dozen young men standing in line vying for her attention. Her dream had always been to go and meet *the one*. The strong, decisive gentleman who would fight anyone who slighted her in the most casual manner. The hero who would steal her away from the crowded ballroom to a lamplit garden where the two of them would...

Freya's wandering thoughts came to a crashing halt. His eyes were open. He was watching her. Feeling a blush warm her cheeks, she tore her gaze away and looked down at the tangle of Ella's hair resting on her lap. She touched the softness of it. A stray curl wound around her finger, just as the very essence of the child had long ago wound inextricably around her heart.

"Are you *really* engaged to Colonel Dunbar?"

She wasn't about to lie and make the arrangement more than it was. Theirs was no love match. The fact that Pennington was acquainted with the Dacres made no difference.

"We have an understanding. The colonel is my cousin.

After my father is gone, he'll be the next Baron of Torrishbrae. For years, it's been expected that we shall marry."

"But for years, you haven't done it."

"I've never been faced with marriage as a deciding factor in my niece's future."

There…she'd said it, Freya thought. It was out. And she knew she might just as well tell him because if she didn't, Ella would. The little imp asleep on her lap had already decided Captain Pennington was a catch.

He *was* a catch. But only for a young woman with a good name and whose life wasn't a tangle of complications.

"Are you saying that Lady Dacre has demanded that you marry in order to keep your niece?"

"The dowager wants assurance that once my father is gone, I have the protection of a husband as well as the means of supporting Ella," she explained. "I have a small fortune of my own, but much of the Sutherland worth is tied up in our land. The estate and all the property that goes with it will be inherited by my cousin."

"So, you're marrying him to keep your own property."

"I'll do anything to keep Ella."

The child stirred. Freya looked down, making sure that their conversation hadn't awakened her. The little girl's steady breathing told her she was still asleep.

"She's right. You are a bloody martyr."

Freya's gaze snapped up to his face and she frowned. "How can you say that when you don't know me?"

"I can say that because I know that family. My parents have an estate in Hertfordshire. They're neighbors, in a sense," he explained. "It was in the duke's character to control and manipulate lives. He *required* martyr's blood.

Lady Dacre's demand sounds very much of the same style as her late husband's. Do what I say or else."

Freya now realized his words had been spoken out of sympathy, and a sense of relief flowed through her, knowing his opinion of the dowager.

"Is she Fredrick's daughter?" he asked softly, his gaze falling on the tousled head in her lap.

Unexpectedly, relief turned to warmth. It wasn't so much his words, but the tone in which he delivered them.

Freya knew very little about Ella's father. Apparently, he cut a dashing figure in his company regimentals. Her sister fell in love with him after the two met at a ball in Edinburgh. Less than a month later, they eloped and were married at Gretna Green. It was all very romantic. Unfortunately, his family had other marital plans for him, but he didn't care. He sent his bride home to Torrishbrae when he returned to fight the French on the Peninsula. And the product of their passionate love affair now lay curled up in her arms.

"She is his daughter," Freya whispered before meeting his gaze again. "Did you know him well?"

"Well enough," he said. "I was a year or so older, but we spent time in each other's company growing up."

"My father and I never met him. Not even once. Nor did Ella," she told him. "I'd love to hear any stories that you could share. She has so many questions, and I don't know how to answer her."

"I'd be happy to, if I can."

The captain's gaze dropped to her lap again, and she looked down and found Ella's eyes open.

Freya wasn't her mother, but she'd been right there with Lucy when Ella entered into the world. And from that first day, she had cared for the infant, loved and celebrated every step, and worried over every bump and bruise. She didn't know if she was capable of putting into words how much she loved Ella.

"Did you have a good sleep?" she asked, caressing her niece's silky cheek.

"Can I look out the window?"

There was no gradual waking up. From the moment Ella opened her eyes, regardless of where and when, she was an unleashed storm. She scrambled over Freya's lap to the window. But that wasn't good enough. Squirming and using her arms and legs, she pushed and made more room for herself.

Her intentions were immediately clear, for Freya found herself sliding along the seat until she was directly across from the captain.

"I apologize," she whispered. "When you agreed to escort us to Baronsford, you couldn't have known you'd be conveying a kraken and its minions."

His smile made her stomach flip deliciously. The confined space of the carriage left nowhere for either of them to go.

"Kraken?" he replied. "I would have said she's a very different mythic creature...a winged one generally armed with a bow and arrow."

A bump on the road pushed his long legs against hers. They each tried to adjust their seats, but the only choice was to tuck her feet in next to his.

"Does your brother, the Lord Justice, make a habit of assigning you such difficult tasks?"

"No more talk of this trip being a hardship," he said softly, his striking eyes surveying her face. "I'm extremely pleased that I'm able to be of service."

His charm was more lethal than his looks. Freya felt

her cheeks warm and tried to slide back toward Ella with no success.

She searched for something to say. Anything to ease the tension gripping her.

"You're stationed in the Highlands?"

"This past year I've been attached to the 93rd Regiment of Foot."

"The Sutherland Highlanders?" she asked, knowing a bit about them. They were located in a wild region of mountains north of Torrishbrae. Most of the soldiers and officers came from the lands of Sutherland, Ross, Caithness, the Orkneys, and the Shetlands.

"I'm an officer in the Royal Engineers, building roads and bridges. My orders there are temporary."

"A necessity…" She couldn't finish the sentence as a bump and a leap of the carriage pressed her leg intimately against his. They were far too close. "As you can see, we desperately need someone of your talent here."

A woolen shawl she'd draped on her lap fell to the floor. He fetched it and spread it over her knees. She whispered a word of thanks at the considerate gesture, but their eyes met and a riot of butterflies swarmed within her, banging against her ribs.

She turned her attention quickly to her niece. Sitting cross-legged on the seat, Ella smiled back at them.

"All of this is boring. Can you please continue with the conversation you were having about my father while I was pretending to be asleep?"

Cupid could take a lesson or two from this little one, Penn thought.

Sitting in that coffee room before they came in, he'd already been formulating what he was going to say to his brother, but any complaint regarding this trip to Baronsford was now forgotten.

These two fascinated him. The older one, in particular. Penn contemplated the curve of Freya's lips and the dimple in her cheek as she played a game of push and shove with her niece to win more space on the seat. For the briefest of moments, while she was distracted, he gazed at the delicate line of her jaw, the slant of her dark eyes, and the soft curls that invited touching.

A true beauty. But what made Miss Freya Sutherland even more striking was her complete lack of awareness of just how alluring she was.

"You are taking too much room, fairy child." She tickled her niece. "Move over."

"I need this much space," Ella complained, swinging her legs around and taking control of most of the seat.

Freya's laughter was as natural as a spring-fed brook. "And I need you to ride up top with Dougal. You'll get so cold that you'll be begging to come inside again for just a wee wedge of space on this seat."

"You wouldn't do that."

"She might not, but by Saint Duthac, you know *I* would, Miss Ella Dacre," Shona growled, having been awakened by the commotion.

As the nurse and the child engaged in their battle of wits, Penn watched Freya try to adjust her legs to avoid the constant contact with his body. But it was no use. There was nowhere to go. And frankly, he had no complaints.

A sharp bump in the road bounced them all, and Freya's immediate response was to reach for Ella and stop the child from being thrown from the seat. Penn, in turn, reached across as Freya herself nearly toppled off.

His hands lingered on her waist, and a momentary scent of jasmine filled his head. But the magic ended abruptly when she sat back, once again gathering her hands and feet. He smiled at the blush gently coloring her cheeks.

"About Captain Dacre," she said in a rush. "You were going to tell us something about Ella's father before."

The suggestion was timely. Staring at Freya, inhaling her scent, and touching her waist only served to provoke the wrong kinds of thoughts in him, considering the situation and the people he was traveling with. He found himself calculating how long it had been since he'd enjoyed a woman's company.

"Do I *look* like him?" Ella asked, directing her question toward Penn.

"I'd have to say your beauty comes from your mother's side of the family. But there are other similarities you share with your father that are indisputable."

The vulnerability showing on the child's face was impossible to miss. The stare, the silence, the breathless expectation. Penn immediately felt the importance of the present moment. He was giving this five-year-old her first impression of a father she'd never seen.

"He was sharp-witted and quick as a kite. Of course, I really only knew him when we were young men, but even then Dacre was capable of making us laugh."

"Do you mean he was always funny?" Ella asked.

"Only when it was called for," he replied. "Your father understood when to be funny and when to be serious."

He stole a glance at Freya and saw her nod. There was a great deal that Penn wasn't about to share. Tales about

Ella's grandfather's loveless severity and his harsh attitudes about duty before love and even before family. These were things Ella didn't need to hear. Neither did she need to know that Dacre made it his life's goal from early on to rebel against his father's wishes in whatever directives were issued. And he often had the stripes and bruises to show for it.

"Was he tall?" Ella wanted to know.

"Indeed. He was quite tall."

"How tall?"

"Nearly as tall as I am."

"Did he have hair on top of his head?"

"He had a thick head of hair, as I recall."

"Did he love his dogs? More than his bloody valet, I mean?"

"Like her grandfather," Freya offered, making sure Penn understood the source of Ella's colorful questions.

"Yes, he loved his dogs."

"What were their names?"

Penn wracked his brain. He couldn't name Dacre's brothers and sisters, never mind his dogs. "He had one named Marlowe that he particularly loved."

"That's a funny name. What did Marlowe look like?"

"He was very big. He was brown and had a black face. He was very gentle, as I recall."

"Was my father fat?"

"No," Penn said, trying to keep a straight face. "Not fat."

"Was his belly as big as Grandfather's?"

He couldn't laugh. She was serious, expecting an answer. "I don't know your grandfather, but your father had no belly. He was fit. Very active."

"Did my father like to smoke for hours and hours and

stare off at the hills, barely saying a word except for things like, 'Go and play by the river. There's a particularly slippery rock in the middle...' or something of the sort?"

"Ella..." Freya admonished, trying to contain her smile.

"No, your father didn't smoke when I knew him."

"When he fell asleep by the fire, did he make smells so terrible that even his dogs went off into the kitchens?"

"Ella, that will do," her aunt said, barely able to get the words out.

With the subtle trace of a smile on her lips, the little girl surveyed her audience, pausing at each face, looking for the reaction. Once she realized her spectators weren't howling, she changed tack. "Could he draw? Or paint?"

Penn considered that. "I would assume he did."

"Could he sing or play the pianoforte?"

"I believe he did, though I'm not certain. We were lads, and we spent a great deal of our free time hunting and fishing and riding. Would you like me to tell you about that?"

Ella squinched up her face. She clearly had little interest in any of those details.

"Was he a good dancer?" she persisted.

Penn looked at the dimple in Freya's cheek as she tried to stifle her smile and turned her face to look out the window.

"I never danced with him, so I don't know."

Shona snorted and then held a kerchief to her nose. Freya turned further, hiding her face as she searched the horizon for something. Penn scratched his jaw and cheek, trying to look thoughtful.

"I'm not being funny. I need to know."

The falter in the child's voice dashed any amusement Penn was feeling. Freya was already sliding across the seat and pulling her niece into her lap. Ella showed no tears, only a trembling chin as she fixed her large brown eyes on him.

"My parents met at a ball. They danced all night and they loved each other. Then I was born," Ella told him. "I need to know if he was a good dancer, because I know my mama was a good dancer."

"Your father was a very good dancer," he said gently.

Ella turned her attention to Freya. "We're going to a ball. You can't dance with a good dancer. You can't. I've changed my mind. You can marry Colonel Richard. You don't love him, and you said he's not a good dancer. That way, you won't go away like Mama did."

❅   3   ❅

THEY'D COVERED half the distance to Inverness, and Freya was relieved when Captain Pennington told them he didn't intend to travel through the night. He ordered the driver to stop just outside of Tain at the grey stone inn. She was familiar with this area of the Highlands and the persisting pilgrimage appeal of St. Duthac's around Advent, so she was not surprised when they were told that there was only one remaining room available for the travelers. Freya, Ella, and Shona would share the room while the men found places to sleep in the tavern and the stables.

Their stop here was to be brief. With so few hours of daylight, the captain wanted to be on the road again long before the sun rose. Ella gave her no trouble and fell fast asleep as soon as they settled into the room. Shona joined them after sharing a supper with her husband.

"Dougal said to tell you that he asked around at the stables. No one's seen a traveler matching Colonel

Dunbar's description stopping here ahead of us. Of course, there are other places in Tain that he could go and ask."

Freya shook her head. "There's no saying he'd stop here at all. We don't even know if he's behind us or ahead of us. The only thing that gives me any peace of mind is that he knows our destination." She picked up the letter that she'd written to her cousin after Ella fell asleep. "Just in case, I am leaving this with the innkeeper downstairs."

She looked across the snug room at the precious face of her sleeping niece.

"*Siuthad*, mistress. Go. She won't be out of my sight."

Freya wasn't about to tell her maid, but leaving the letter for the colonel was only an excuse to go downstairs. She knew Captain Pennington was there in the taproom, and she needed to see him. They hadn't had a chance to speak freely after Ella's emotional outburst, and there was a great deal that needed explaining. For however long it took to reach Baronsford, the captain was stuck with them. It was her duty to warn him, she told herself, to explain what prompted the child's reaction.

As she paused at the top of the staircase and ran a hand down the skirt of her traveling dress, Freya knew deep down that all of that was, in part, an excuse too. She *wanted* to see him. His looks, his manner, the subtle clues he'd given her that indicated he sympathized with her situation, all of it appealed to her. And his timing could not be better. She could use an ally when they arrived at Baronsford.

When she reached the bottom of the steps, she found the smoky taproom to be more crowded than she expected. Working men milled about and filled every table, playing cards and throwing dice at hazard. At one table, a rambunctious trio were cheering on rivals in a game of nine-men's morris. In a far corner, a drunken group were crooning a Highland song of a maid lost to the fairy king. Finally, the innkeeper appeared through a cellar door, and Freya handed him the letter with her instructions.

The man walked off, and she moved across the room. But it was difficult to find Captain Pennington in the thick of all the activity. Then, as she stopped and stood on her toes looking for him, someone looped an arm around her waist and roughly pulled her around.

"And where, my bonnie jo, have ye been?"

The smell of whiskey and pig manure nearly knocked Freya out. She glared into the flushed face and drooping unfocused eyes.

"Release me," she snapped. "And I mean *now*."

"But I've been a-waiting for you all this dreary night, lassie," the young man slurred in Gaelic, taking hold of her arms as he tried to keep his balance. "Who'd have thought a mornin' star like you would fall to Earth here in T—"

"You will take your hands off me this instant," she scolded fiercely. "Or by God and his angels, I'll give you a bruising that you'll be telling your children about for years to come. *If* you're able to have any."

"Aye, an *aingeal*." He started to smile but quickly appeared to change his mind. His eyes opened wide, and he dropped his hands from her arms. He stepped back and turned away, mumbling, "Sorry, mistress. I thought ye were...I thought I..."

Freya watched as he slunk off like a whipped dog. Her father always commended her for her manner of no-

nonsense strength, and the men around Torrishbrae—whether they be tenants or servants or locals—treated her with deference. But the lack of fight demonstrated by her pig farming harasser was impressive.

Still, she wasn't going to press her luck. Perhaps, she decided, tonight wasn't the ideal time to speak with Captain Pennington. She turned back toward the steps, only to find his chest a hand's breadth from her face.

The flutter of pleasure came with no warning. She backed up a step and looked behind her where her would-be suitor had disappeared, and turned again to the captain.

"How long have you been standing here?" she asked, daring herself to look up into his handsome face. He'd shed his scarlet coat, and the white shirt beneath his waistcoat was unbuttoned at the throat.

"Long enough to learn that laying a hand on you without an invitation is done at great peril."

Freya bit her bottom lip to stop from smiling and met his gaze. "Show me the look that made the man run."

"Only if you show me yours."

A barmaid carrying pitchers of ale bumped Freya from behind, pushing her into Captain Pennington's chest. His arm wrapped protectively around her, drawing her away from the commotion behind her. She took a deep breath, feeling a thrill take hold deep in her belly.

"Come with me," he murmured, bringing his mouth close.

His deep voice and his breath tickling her ear were enough to start Freya's senses dancing with pleasure. On the small of her back, she felt the warmth of his hand through the material of her dress. Using his great height and body to shield her, they moved easily through the crowded room.

Freya wasn't accustomed to this feeling of being looked after. In her whole life, she'd never been the object of this kind of attentiveness.

They reached a table in the corner, curtained off from the rest of the room. He ushered her inside. "Do you mind joining me here?"

"Not at all, Captain."

A large settle against the wall had already been arranged with a blanket for him to sleep on, though his long legs would certainly be requiring a chair to extend the makeshift bed.

She glanced around at the table. Several chairs were drawn up to it, and he picked up his greatcoat and a leather travel bag from one of them and tossed the items on the settle. A cold, damp wind was howling through the cracks around a shuttered window.

"I'm sorry you have to sleep here," she said.

"My driver said there are better accommodations above the stables, but this is just fine."

"Why didn't you take them?"

"With this crowd of ne'er-do-wells? I didn't want to be too far from you."

Freya was touched by his protectiveness.

He held a chair for her, and she sat. The remains of his meal lay on the table.

"Can I order you some supper?" he asked. "I wouldn't recommend the pigeon pie, but the oysters are surprisingly fresh."

"Thank you, but no. I took dinner with Ella."

"Then perhaps you'll take a glass with me. This elder wine is quite good."

She wanted to but wondered if she should. Dulling her senses, alone in the company of someone with his looks and charm, might not be a good idea.

After receiving another cup from the barmaid, Pennington closed the curtain. "I'd prefer we not invite any of these unsavory characters in," he said.

Freya knew he was the safest person she could be with in this taproom. He poured her a cup of wine from the pitcher and slid it toward her.

"How did you know I was down here?" she asked. "You were quick to come to my aid."

"The tenor of the noise out there changed. I knew the moment you came down the steps," he said. "I've spent too much time in the company of soldiers. I know too well the sounds of the taproom."

She looked over her shoulder at the closed curtain and listened. The hubbub and hum of voices rose and fell. Words were mostly unintelligible, but the singers had been reduced to one voice entertaining the others.

"Is anything happening now?"

"Nothing but a crowd of men looking for an hour of leisure. Some have drunk too much ale or whiskey, and all of them are tired from their labors."

"And how was it different when I came down?"

"Let me just say that I knew."

She turned back to the table and found him watching her. The dim light of the single guttering candle in the curtained-off space was a blessing, as she felt the warmth of a blush spreading up her neck into her face.

In preparing herself for this journey, Freya had imagined it would be all hardship and sorrow. She knew what lay at the end of it. Even if her cousin showed up and Lady Dacre was amenable to allowing Ella's living arrangements to remain as they were, Freya still had to face up to her own future. She was no fool. She knew her marriage would be a sham and, in the end, a wretched failure.

And now, here she was, sitting across from this man. Captain Pennington was handsome enough to make her heart throb incessantly and considerate enough to even give up his comforts.

"I am sorry about today and Ella's outburst," she said, watching him refill his cup of wine. "She is far too aware of things for her age. Unfortunately, she knows too much and worries even more."

"She's afraid of losing you."

"She's very alert to my emotions. She recognizes my concerns, and that only adds to her fears."

Freya stared at the dark liquid in her cup. Ella was an uncommon child, and her upbringing thus far could be considered by some as unconventional. Since before she could talk, she'd been treated like an adult. She was always in the company of older people. Hand in hand, they had experienced life and its obstacles together, even as Freya herself learned to deal with them. She was beginning to think she should have sheltered Ella more.

"When did your sister pass away?"

The captain's question brought Freya's attention back to him. "A week after Ella was born."

"That was a large responsibility to be left with."

She shrugged. "Lucy was my only sister, and Ella's father was fighting the French. I needed to step in and take charge of the bairn. I was glad to do it. But I wasn't alone. I had my father."

"How old were you then?"

"Seventeen."

His gaze moved over her face, and she picked up the

cup of wine, unable to stand the intensity of his perusal. She took a swallow, savoring the warm liquid.

"You were a young woman at the very beginning of your own adult life. You became your niece's guardian at an age when most lasses would have been fussing over their social calendar or the contents of their hope chest."

"I was a young woman faced with the loss of my sister," she corrected, still feeling after all these years the pain of Lucy's death. They were only two years apart. She'd lost not only a sister but her best friend. "I was willing and able to shoulder what I knew to be my duty. And, I'll be honest, that's what those first days were to me. An obligation. But that quickly changed. I fell in love with my sister's precious daughter. Ella was a blessing. A gift."

"You were plucked from your own life and dropped into your sister's. That had to be difficult. The adjustment, I mean."

The captain had a point. She wouldn't deny it. Freya still had not forgotten the dreams of her youth. She recalled that one day she had been trying to decide between green material or gold for a dress and another day, a month later, she was frantic with worry over Ella not sleeping and not taking to the wet nurse. She'd kept the village doctor busy at all hours of the day and night.

"You had to grow up fast."

"Many a lass of seventeen is a mother, Captain."

"That's true. But it doesn't change what happened to you."

"I did grow up in a hurry," she admitted. "The fact is, I hardly noticed it. But who can truly tell what the future holds? Few go through life along some smooth and protected path, emerging unscathed," she said. "To my thinking, the courage of a person is tested not only in battle, but in how well they react and recover when life knocks them to the side with unexpected blows."

A momentary hush fell between them. His eyes fixed on hers. The thought ran through Freya's mind as he gazed at her that this man was truly seeing her. Not the exterior of a woman, but the person she'd become since taking charge of her niece. And this unsettled her. She felt exposed, vulnerable, and drawn to him. No one, including her father, really understood the transformation her life had undergone.

She searched for something to say to break the silence. "My father tells me I lecture too much. I apologize if I've come across as some didactic old crone, Captain."

"You can call me Penn. That's what my friends call me."

She hesitated, unsure of how this would sound to others.

"And to my family, I'm Gregory. I'd be very pleased if we could curtail this formality."

"Gregory it is then," she said quietly. "And pray, call me Freya. That's how my family refers to me. And you already know Ella's name for me."

"Fie." He smiled. "Like a fairy. You're Ella's magical keeper, spreading your unseen wings around the little pixy, keeping her secure from the world."

His voice spread over her like poetry. Freya's face caught fire, and her insides were like the candle on the table, melting in this man's presence.

He added some wine to his cup. He charmed her, enthralled her. There was so much that she wanted to know about him, questions that she had. But she had no right to ask. Where her heart was straying, her mind could not allow her to go.

Freya forced her attention back to the clatter of dice and the hum of voices beyond the curtain. Sitting across from each other at the table, there was nowhere else she could look but at him. And there was nothing nearly as interesting to think of but the man before her.

"May I ask a personal question?" he asked.

"Everything we've been talking about tonight has been personal, Captain...I mean, Gregory." She took another sip and prepared herself.

His smile was lethal. It reached his magical eyes, and Freya's heart began a new dance in her chest.

"Why didn't you marry someone before now?" he asked.

"You mean to someone other than the colonel?"

He shrugged and swirled the wine in his cup.

"Well..."

"And I want an honest answer," he pressed. "We are talking as friends here. No hesitating to sort through your thoughts or weigh the consequences of your answer."

"Is that how friends converse?" She laughed. "With no consideration of the consequences of their words?"

"Well, let's say for this question, you need not fear being misunderstood."

Friends. She repeated the word in her mind. She'd never had a man refer to her as a friend. Very well. Having such a defined relationship made their situation—their close proximity in traveling in the same carriage and the time they'd be spending with each other on the road—far more comfortable. It also helped cool the forbidden fancies of her heart.

"I've never left Torrishbrae for the expressed purpose

of finding a potential husband," she said flatly. "I've had no time for the social world of London or even Edinburgh. That is why I've never married. And I have no regrets. My life has been so full. Ella has been my whole world."

"And now?" he asked, sitting back from the table. His face lay half in shadow. "When you consider the difficulties you're facing presently, do you have any regrets?"

"As I said earlier, I'm certain the rumors that you heard about my cousin were a mistake. I am counting on him to hold up his part of the bargain."

"I've only known you a short time, but I know that in this bargain, you are being greatly shortchanged."

Freya was not intimidated by his fierce expression of honesty. Her father was famous for it. Living with it for her whole life instilled in her a toughness and an ability to see the world clearly.

"There is no changing the fact that he will be the next baron of Torrishbrae. By marrying him, I will have Ella. That's all I seek."

"You will have Ella but it is naïve to think that Dunbar's disposition and how he conducts his affairs won't affect your life," he persisted. "The man is a known gambler. An opportunist. One who will behave in an ungentlemanly manner if it will turn a situation to his favor. He is—"

"He is my cousin, Captain," she interrupted. She knew all of this and more. But for the past month, she'd stewed over this, discussed it with her father. "I've looked at this from every possible angle, and my options are gone. If I am to keep Ella, I must take whatever future presents itself with this man."

Standing, she started out and then stopped. Freya

didn't want to leave with hard feelings. She valued their conversation and the friendship that seemed to be emerging between them.

"Thank you, Gregory, for the chance to speak my mind," she said softly. "But for better or worse, Colonel Dunbar is the only possibility I have."

4

PENN REMEMBERED someone saying the best preparation for traveling in the Highlands in the winter was making out your will. With the ice on the road and only six hours of daylight at this time of the year, the dangers were evident. But he wasn't going to keep a child cooped up in a carriage from well before sunrise to well after dark.

He glanced up at the sunless sky as he walked across the inn's stable yard. Their horses were being fed and rested. They still had hours to travel today, but it was already growing darker.

Behind the stable, a glen of fir trees sloped down from the low rise that the coast road had been following. As they'd approached from the north, he'd seen a wide mill pond extending out from the woodland. It was the perfect place for Ella to stretch her little legs and tire herself with exercise.

Making his way down through the clusters of pine and spruce, he saw no trace of Freya and her niece. With the trees cutting off the wind, a muffled silence surrounded him. He reached a fork in the path and stopped, listening for some sign of them. Hearing a whisper of laughter, he followed the sound and soon found the frozen pond, nestled into the snow-covered meadow beyond the glen.

The nursemaid sat on a log with her back to him. Penn's eyes fixed on Freya and her niece as the two, holding each other's hands, spun in a circle on the smooth ice.

Listening to the happy laughter, he stood and watched what seemed to be a competition as to who would slip and fall first.

"Hold on tight," Freya yelled as they picked up momentum, both their feet moving faster and faster as they whirled about each other.

"I'm going to fall," Ella screamed, laughing.

"I won't let you go."

Penn watched Freya. The hood of her blue cloak was tossed back, her light brown curls fighting to be free of their bonds. The ruby lips and cold-reddened cheeks illuminated the grey countryside, and he thought that if he could paint perfection, it would start with this vision.

Their conversation in the taproom kept coming back to him throughout the night and this morning. Her words about courage and accepting responsibility. Freya was mature beyond her years...and selfless in a way that many never achieved. He thought of his own family. His mother, Millicent. His sister Jo, and his two younger sisters. How pleased they'd be to meet a woman who embodied the same values they prized.

"Slow down. I am going to faint," Freya called out as the two giggled and laughed.

When it was safe, she let go of her niece's hand, then

promptly bent down and sat on the ice, holding a hand to her forehead.

"I win. I win."

Penn forced himself to step onto the edge of the ice, where he could be seen.

Ella saw him first. She waved excitedly and then promptly slipped, sitting hard on the ice next to her aunt.

"Thank you for stopping, Captain," Shona said, standing when she saw him. "Miss Ella needed this."

"I believe you're right."

Anytime Freya tried to get to her feet, Ella pushed her down. What had been a spinning circle was now an amusing wrestling match.

"Get this fiend away from me," Freya cried out, laughing breathlessly and reaching a hand toward them.

He wanted to be on the ice with them, be part of their game, and be included in their camaraderie. Penn started across the pond toward the two giggling females.

"Perhaps these will help," he said as he drew near. He held out two pairs of well-used skates he'd borrowed from the innkeeper. His own pair was tucked under his arm.

Ella's eyes lit up. "Thank you," she chirped, taking the smallest blades from him. She darted away, slipping constantly but keeping her balance until she reached the log where Shona sat waiting to help her.

Freya was struggling to rise.

"May I?" he said, leaning down to help.

She slid her gloved hand into his as he pulled her up. She slipped as she tried to find her balance and stumbled against him. The scent of jasmine filled his head again as he held her tight against his chest.

"Are these for me?" she asked, drawing away.

He handed her the skates, and Penn thought her

enthusiasm surpassed the child's. She leaned down right there, trying to put them on.

Watching her, he strapped on his skates. He guessed the spinning was still affecting her, for she was having difficulty.

"Allow me." He dropped to one knee before her.

She started to say something but then stopped as he held her ankle and lifted her boot. She put a hand on his shoulder. Making a short work of it, he moved on to the other.

Ella skated up behind her aunt and bumped her. Both of Freya's hands landed on his shoulders as blue cloth swirled about him.

"I'm so sorry. That fairy child is going to pay for this."

The scent of her, the feel of her coat and skirts, and the trusting intimacy of her hold on him had his senses reeling. Done with her skates, he pushed upright only to have Ella swoop by, grazing her aunt with another pass. Freya clung to his greatcoat as he straightened up.

This close, her breath mingled with his, and their eyes locked for a long moment. Then, out of the corner of his eye, he saw Ella coming at them a third time. Grasping Freya by the waist, he swung her around to avoid the assault and the enthusiastic child raced past.

"I see you've skated before," he called after her.

"Oh, yes," Ella responded happily, gliding off as if she were born on ice. "We can skate for a thousand miles on our river when it freezes."

"A thousand miles?" he asked, injecting humor in his tone as Freya pushed away from him.

"At least a thousand." She smiled, following her niece and showing the same proficiency on skates.

He followed a couple of strides behind them, appreciating the opportunity to observe the graceful way Freya's body moved and swayed as she turned and danced across the ice. Sometime during their conversations yesterday and this morning, a tie had begun to form—like a lifeline fired from the shore to a foundering vessel—connecting her to him. He'd begun to care about Freya and her situation. He worried about the tumble and fall that was ahead. He feared the outcome. He knew Ella would be provided for—by the Dacre family or the Sutherlands—but Freya's future was at risk.

Her sparkling brown eyes sought him out, making certain he was nearby, and he relished the feeling that she also recognized the link they'd established.

As they skated, the aunt and niece repeatedly reached for each other, linking arms and spinning and gliding off. This was as easy for them as walking.

Penn felt a pleasurable warmth well up within him when the object of his gaze extended a gloved hand toward him.

"Do you need help keeping up, Captain?"

He didn't, but for the life of him, he wasn't about to miss this opportunity. Penn took her hand and drew up beside her. Effortlessly, they found their rhythm and began to circle the pond, trailing the mulberry-coated elf who moved ahead of them and around them, gleefully taunting them for being so slow.

"Can I ask you a question?" Freya asked.

"Please."

"I always assumed men joined the military to fight."

"So you don't consider engineering a gallant or worthwhile profession?" he suggested.

"Quite the opposite," she said quickly. "I find it fascinating. Many Sutherland men who were fortunate enough to survive the war on the continent came home damaged in body and spirit. Their sole task for many years had been to battle the Spaniards and the French. Since then, many have struggled with adjusting to the peace. They can no longer farm the land of their ancestors. But you're a builder. Engineering as a life focused on designing and improving the world of tomorrow."

Her eyes shone with interest when they met his.

"I am fascinated to know what made you decide on this path."

Her curiosity intrigued him. Her attitude, so buoyant and positive, warmed him.

"I believe you know about my older brother."

"I know of Viscount Greysteil, the Lord Justice in Edinburgh," she said. "But only a wee bit."

"Well, he was always taller, wider in shoulders, quicker to fight. He's a powerful force in person. From his youth, he's been a man who leaves an impression. As his younger brother, I knew almost from childhood that if I chose to follow in his steps I'd be lost in his shadow."

"So you decided to make your own way," she said, understanding.

"As a gentleman, I had few paths open to me. I could buy an estate, or pursue a profession in the law or the church, but those did not appeal to me. I could see the world is changing, with new innovations emerging every day: steam engines and railways, improved methods of road and bridge building, and machinery that has radically changed the way we mine the earth and manufacture our cloth. We're at the dawn of a new age, and I was always drawn to that. Once I decided to pursue this passion, I realized the army would provide a valuable training ground. And it has, though the war against Napoleon made for a costly education."

"What exactly does an engineer do during war?"

"Everything from creating and maintaining transport routes for the armies, securing water supplies, preparing defensive positions before battle..." His voice trailed off as he considered how far he'd come from those bloody scenes.

"Everything that the soldiers need to survive," she surmised, drawing him out of his reverie. "A vital profession, Captain, in war and in peace."

He didn't have a chance to respond, for Ella was pulling her aunt away for a turn on the ice.

Penn watched them go and glided after the two. The surface was as smooth as glass, and for a moment he closed his eyes and lifted his face to the sky, reveling in the cheerful calm that had descended upon him, infusing his mind and body with a sense of well-being. Freya's interest and her understanding of his career were a surprise and no doubt prompted this state of mind.

When was the last time that he'd felt such peace? Could he remember any time in the past decade when he gave no care to where he had to be, what he had to do, or what plan he needed to set in motion for the morrow?

He couldn't, and perhaps because of this, he was happy. Unexpectedly happy.

Penn opened his eyes and saw his companion at his side again. Freya's bright face and shining eyes would have drawn the envy of the angels.

Catching him staring, she linked her arm with his.

"I'd like to apologize for last night," she told him when Ella rushed off toward the nursemaid.

"For what?"

"For sounding very much like a martyr. For deserting you as soon as you started talking about my complicated and troubling arrangement," she said in a whisper with a glance at her niece, who was now unsuccessfully attempting to pull Shona onto the ice. "I didn't mean any disrespect."

A chill wind, scented with the salty sea smell, swirled in around them, stirring up wisps of snow, and his thoughts darkened. "I felt no such intention in anything you said. And I hope you know my words were spoken out of concern."

He was still concerned, today even more than yesterday. The more time he spent with these two, the more he knew how wrong it would be for them to fall under the influence of a man whose sole interest was undoubtedly to enrich himself through the marriage. Dunbar was infamous both for his gambling debts and for his shadowy dealings with women.

"You know the Dacre family and you know something about me," she stated. "I'd like your honest answer, as one...as one friend to another. Disregarding the superior fortune that they undoubtedly possess relative to that of a Scottish baron, do you think Ella would be better raised by them or by us?"

There was no hesitation in his answer. "Without even knowing your father, you are unquestionably better suited."

"And if you add the enormous wealth and influence of that family to your consideration?"

"Still you," he said. Penn's gaze drifted over to where Ella, having given up, was now sitting on the log beside Shona, swinging her feet as she chattered with her nurse. "You've done a wonderful job with her. She's a delight. So full of life. Happy, intelligent. She's a brave little creature."

"Too brave." Freya smiled.

"She has a strong spirit," he said, pressing her hand on his arm. "A spirit that I believe she gets from you."

"She is a great deal like me in many ways. And she is also very much like my father." Her smile dimmed slightly. "My sister was Ella's age and I was a couple of years younger when our mother died, so my father has extensive experience in raising little girls. And Ella and her grandfather dote on each other, despite their wicked tongues."

Penn had no doubt the Sutherlands' loving care would be far better than the slew of nannies and governesses Lady Dacre would assemble to break Ella's spirit and mold her into a "perfect" lady.

But there was still the matter of Dunbar. Penn had to agree with Freya's belief that the rumors of the colonel marrying the Caithness woman could be false. Now that he thought of it, what better excuse for putting off all the people he owed money to? From their perspective, what could be more attractive than him marrying an heiress with ready cash? The Caithness money could easily pay off the man's debts. Of course sooner or later, they would catch up to his lie and by then he hoped to take possession of Torrishbrae, either through marriage or inheritance.

Dunbar was poison for Freya and Ella, no matter how one looked at it.

"What if you were to speak honestly with Lady Dacre?" he suggested. "Perhaps she would give you time to find a more suitable husband, one you could care for and respect."

Her nose wrinkled and she shook her head. He recalled seeing this same expression on Ella's face when he jokingly asked her if she'd care for some cabbage with her porridge this morning.

"I'm years past such fanciful delusions. I'm set in my ways."

"Twenty-two years of age," he teased. "So old!"

"If fate turns its back on me and my cousin fails to appear, for whatever reason, and if, after substantial groveling, Lady Dacre grants me some time, where am I going to meet this suitable husband?" she asked, "It's not like I'll be leaving Torrishbrae, at the age of twenty-two or twenty-three, for a season of husband-hunting in London. And even if I were able to manage that—which I won't— what man would want a bride who brings with her a five-year-old 'daughter' who is as unpredictable as a summer storm? And a father who relies on her living in the Highlands to help manage his affairs?"

A summer storm? Ella and Freya together were like the first warm breezes of spring after the bitter cold of winter. But Penn knew there was a great deal of truth in what she said. He had many friends, and he'd heard enough stories of engagements and marriages. Many men of rank and wealth maintained limited and superficial views of what they believed made for a good marriage partner. Wealth, a good family with a history of male offspring, and an uncomplicated personal history.

Giving up on him answering, she shrugged and smiled sadly.

"I'm resigned to what I must do." She unlinked her arm and moved away. "The only purpose of having a man in my life would be to retain custody of Ella. Nothing else."

"Nothing else?" he repeated, coming to stop in front of her. "What about companionship and friendship? Love and romance and passion? Don't you think you deserve to experience the same breathless happiness that your sister experienced when she eloped with Fredrick Dacre? Don't you want to have a child of your own? Don't you wonder what it's like to love a man?"

Penn didn't know where this outpouring of emotion came from. His gaze fixed on her face. She was staring at him, her eyes wide. Her lips parted slightly, quick puffs of breath escaping.

At that moment, more than anything in the world, he wanted to kiss those lips. And Dunbar be damned.

$$\text{❧ 5 ☙}$$

THIS WAS NOT the time for confusion or second-guessing, Freya thought.

Her conversation with Gregory had continued during the ensuing time spent in the carriage, though she tried to focus her questions on his past and the career that appeared to match his personality perfectly.

She was fascinated with him. As a second son, he was exceptional in that he'd not wasted his life, like so many of his peers, on drinking and gambling. He'd made his own decisions, found a path to happiness, and carved out an independence that was so rare, considering his family's rank and status.

The captain's enthusiasm for his projects even drew the attention of Ella and Shona as they rumbled southward. The places he'd seen, the canals and bridges and roads they'd built, and the adventures and obstacles he'd faced enthralled them.

Gregory Pennington was confusing everything,

however, with those stories of his life and his kindness and his sweet words and his handsome face. He was muddying waters that had never been crystal clear to begin with.

Well, it couldn't work, this...whatever it was between them. Attraction and foolishness.

A splash in the tub broke up her thoughts.

Ella, up to her armpits in the bath, was busily sailing a carved toy boat—bearing the princess—across the German Sea to the shores of Norway where she was about to do battle with a wicked colonel who was holding the prince in a tower. From the look of things, the wicked colonel had taken to the sea on a bar of soap for the epic engagement.

Freya soaked the wash towel in the warm water and draped it over the little commander's shoulders. Shona was sitting in a chair on the far side of the hearth, stitching a seam on one of Ella's gloves.

As she absently stirred the soapy water, Freya's mind drifted back to her current situation. The outcome was as predictable as Ella's drama. Gregory was the son of an earl, Lord Aytoun. She was a baron's daughter. And a Highlander. Though Aytoun was not a duke, the family was extremely wealthy, powerful, and well-connected in England and Scotland. They traveled in the same society as the Dacres. Gregory's brother, Viscount Greysteil, was a Lord Justice in Edinburgh and a war hero. Baronsford, their home in Scotland, was one of the grandest castles in the Borders. She'd even seen an etching of it in a book in her father's library.

She was a fool, she told herself, to torment herself with hopes that would never be realized. Captain Pennington was too far out of her reach.

But at the same time, she thought with a sigh of the moment when he'd almost kissed her while they were skating. She'd seen it in his eyes. The battle had been visible in his features, in the way he'd struggled to stop his hands from reaching for her. She'd felt it as certainly as the ice beneath their feet.

His words about passion and love had stirred a deeply buried need inside of her. Freya hadn't known until then how starved she was for a simple kiss. For the lips of the man who made her mind and body catch fire when she was with him. Gregory's kiss.

She knew it would be a kiss that would change her life.

When they weren't together, she thought of him. She relived the words he spoke. The sense of humor he maintained while dealing with Ella's playful antics. The lingering looks he sent her.

Today, as the carriage bumped along, the imp sat beside him as the two worked with charcoal, drawing pictures of Freya. He was a surprisingly good artist. But she'd squirmed and blushed as he stared openly at her eyes and cheeks and lips, moving appraisingly downward over the bodice of her travel dress.

A splash of water yanked her from her reverie. Shona was standing beside the tub.

"I don't want to get out," Ella complained as the nurse tried to convince the child to come out of the warm bath and dress for bed. "The princess still needs to rescue the prince, who had been secretly taken to the Rajah's cave. Five more minutes should do it."

"You said that ten minutes ago," Freya reminded her. "Up you go. Look at your wrinkled fingers. You're already a prune."

Ella studied her fingers. "Grandfather says cock-a-leekie soup's not cock-a-leekie soup without the prunes. He says only a bloody Englishman would think so. Do you think so, Shona?"

"I think you need to watch your language, lassie. And don't go saying things like that in front of the captain, *a chloiseann tú*? Do you hear?"

"Why? Is the captain a bloody Englishman, Fie?"

"He's part English," Freya said. "But Shona's right. You need to stop repeating everything your grandfather says."

As Shona lifted the child out and dried her, Freya placed another log on the fire. Adding hot water to the bath from a pitcher on the hearth, she quickly undressed and climbed into the tub herself.

"These are fine rooms the captain has taken for us all," Shona said, wrapping Ella in the towel and standing her by the fire to stay warm. "Dougal was more than grateful that his lordship insisted on the two of us sleeping in the third bedroom."

"You're right about the captain's kindness. He insisted on me and Ella taking this room, while he's in the smaller bedchamber."

This inn, overlooking Huntly's market cross, was far more elegant than the places they'd stopped their past three nights on the road. The captain had taken the entire apartment on the upper floor where three bedchambers and a large sitting room were at their disposal.

"The captain even took a room for his driver and the groom."

"So I understand," Freya responded, quickly washing her hair.

"Do you want help with that?" Shona asked, pulling a nightgown over Ella's head. "This wee one is going right into that bed."

"No, I'm fine, thank you," she replied, pouring water over her hair.

"I am not sleepy," Ella complained.

"You will be as soon as you close your eyes," Freya told her.

"But I saw a backgammon game on the shelf in the sitting room."

"I'd wager there are games waiting for you when we arrive at Baronsford," she said. "You need to get your sleep. We'll be up early and on the road again."

The shutters on the windows rattled with the wind, a reminder that even with no fresh snow, winter ruled the landscape.

"Will the captain's family like me?" Ella asked, climbing onto the bed.

"I believe they'll love you," Freya said.

"So long as you don't go calling them bloody Englishmen," Shona added.

"Will they let me play games?"

"I think they will. But you'll have to ask nicely, and be on your best behavior."

The nursemaid tucked the child into the bed, and Freya smiled gratefully at her. "You should get some rest too, Shona."

"I think I might just do that, mistress." Bidding them both goodnight, she picked up her sewing and went out.

From where she sat in the tub, Freya had a clear view

of the cherub's face. Her little head lay on her arm. Her eyes struggled to stay open.

Freya thought about getting out, but the warm water and the heat from the fireplace felt too good to waste.

"Is Colonel Richard going to be there with us at Baronsford?" Ella asked.

"I believe so."

When they stopped at Inverness two nights ago, after their skating stop, Dougal had made the rounds of the better inns. Still no sign of her cousin. She had no way of knowing if he was ahead of them or behind them.

"He'll join us at Dundee," Freya said, trying to sound both certain and happy about it. "He'll accompany us to Baronsford from there."

The child yawned. "That's too bad."

"I thought you wanted me to marry him."

"Not anymore," Ella whispered. "I've changed my mind again."

"Have you?" Freya replied softly, sinking into the bath until the water came up to her chin. The image of Gregory Pennington's face out on that frozen pond appeared to her. She'd change her mind too, she thought, if she had the chance.

"I've decided you should marry a good dancer and a good skater," Ella said, closing her eyes. "Ask Captain Pennington. Or I can ask him for you. I know he'll do it."

Penn pushed open the shutter and peered out through the darkness. Occasional breaks in the clouds allowed the moon to shed its light over Huntly's rooftops. Four days they'd been on the road and, despite having to make frequent stops for Ella, they were making excellent progress. The unpredictable Highland weather, though cold, had been cooperating, so far.

Tomorrow night, they'd stop at Aberdeen, he thought, shuttering the window again and going over to the small fireplace. He had an old friend there, a former officer who'd served with him on the Peninsula and later in the Royal Engineers. John Simpson resigned his captain's commission a year ago and was now married and advising on plans for road building and other projects in the coastal area. Penn had received many invitations from him, and he knew Simpson and his wife would be happy to put them up for the night.

Washing up and stripping out of his clothes, Penn lay down in the bed. Staring at the firelight flickering on the surfaces of the rafters overhead, he thought of Freya. He wondered if she noticed how relieved he was every time her queries about her cousin produced blank looks from innkeepers. There'd been no sign of Dunbar along the route thus far. Perhaps the stars had aligned and the scoundrel had actually married one heiress or another.

He knew he had another reason for stopping off at his friend's home in Aberdeen. Simpson's last assignment had been at Fort William, where Dunbar's regiment was posted. His friend was always one to keep in contact with his former colleagues. Perhaps he'd have more information about the colonel.

Freya's marriage to her cousin was wrong. And Penn was prepared to do whatever it was necessary to make her see the grave mistake she'd be making in going through with the ill-advised arrangement.

He considered their arrival at Baronsford. Once they got there, he'd insist on speaking with Lady Dacre on Freya and Ella's behalf. This urgency was nonsense. Freya needed time to settle her future. His thoughts darkened. He hadn't known the eldest son growing up. He was already an adult when Penn was still a child, but the word was that the new duke, haughty and narrow-minded, wasn't much of an improvement over his late father. Still, Penn was ready to go to battle with them. He'd seek his brother Hugh's assistance as to legal proceedings, if need be. Freya didn't need to face these people alone.

The soft knock on the door caught him amid his mental combat. The next sound had him jumping out of bed and pulling on his trousers and shirt. Someone was trying to come in.

Penn crossed the floor and yanked the door open. Outside, the intruder was jumping up, trying to reach the latch.

"What are you doing out of bed?" he asked, looking down at the shivering little bundle.

"I knew you'd be awake," Ella said, stepping back and motioning for him to come with her. "I need your help."

"With what?" he asked, buttoning his shirt. "Where's your aunt?"

"That's what I need help with." She took his hand and started pulling him toward the door of their room.

"What's wrong with her?" he asked, suddenly worried.

"She's fallen asleep in the tub. And I am afraid if she stays there all night she'll end up looking like one of those old apples we feed to the pigs."

"That sounds quite serious." He stopped outside of their bedchamber door. "Why don't you awaken her?"

The little girl made a shocked face and shook her head from side to side. "No, I need *you* to do it."

Penn hid a chuckle behind the pretense of a cough. Beyond this door, Freya was naked and asleep in a tub, and this little matchmaker was mature enough to know he'd be interested in it.

"You should go get Shona. She can awaken her mistress."

Ella again shook her head from side to side, mouthing a big no. "Fie always tells me never to walk into Shona's room when Dougal is there and the door is closed. It's inap...inapppie..."

"Inappropriate?"

She nodded, pushing open the door a little. "You wake her."

"I think your aunt might consider it inappropriate for me to go into her bedchamber and wake her up." He took a step back. "No, I think you're the best person for the job."

As she bit her lip and stared up at him, Penn started worrying. The water Freya was lying in had to be cold. Was there enough wood in the fireplace? She definitely could catch a chill. He decided he should knock loudly and wake her up.

"I'll do it," Ella announced. "But under one condition."

He should have guessed this imp would have a secondary motive. "What?"

"I'll wake her and come back if you'll play a game of backgammon with me."

He looked across the sitting room where she was pointing. A game box sat on a table by the fireplace.

"You know how to play?"

"Grandfather taught me."

"I don't know. We have a full day tomorrow."

"I know it's late and after your bedtime," she responded. "Only one game."

The possibility sprang to Penn's mind that Freya wasn't in any tub, at all, but sound asleep in her bed. This entire thing could be the ploy of the diminutive strategist standing before him.

He pretended a yawn. "It *is* after my bedtime. Maybe we can play a game tomorrow night when we stop at my friend's house."

She crossed her arms, staring up at him. "Fie might not make it till tomorrow if she sleeps in the tub all night."

Penn had never found himself in a standoff with a five-year-old. "My proposition is this. You go and awaken your aunt. If she makes a noise loud enough that I can hear her all the way out here, then I'll tell you a story."

"What kind of a story?"

"A good story that I guarantee you've never heard from your grandfather."

She sent him a skeptical look. "I've heard lots and lots of stories. Thousands of them."

"This one was told to me and my brother and sisters by a woman named Ohenewaa. She was like a grand-mother to us, and she was from Africa."

"Tell me the start of it."

He couldn't believe this lassie. She wasn't about to be cheated.

"Lizard shows tortoise a hidden cave filled with yams." He stopped. "Go awaken her."

She ran into the bedchamber, leaving the door ajar. Not a moment later, Penn heard a splash and Freya's loud gasp. Before he could formulate an image of what had just happened, Ella was back out, closing the door.

"Very well," she said, taking him by the hand and leading him to a settle close to the fire. "I want to hear the rest of it. But what's a yam?"

$\maltese$ *6* $\maltese$

JOLTED AWAKE BY ELLA, Freya stood in the tub, looking dazedly after her escaping niece.

She'd fallen asleep in the bath. When had she ever done that? Never, before tonight.

Pulling her nightgown over her head, Freya hurried to the door leading to the sitting room. She opened it and saw them.

Ella, wrapped in a blanket, was already cuddled beside the captain on a settle. She stood still, leaning against the doorway, incapable of intruding on an experience that she knew was a first. Gregory was the only man outside of the family that she'd ever seen Ella warm up to. The child was listening with rapt attention as he related a story of a land of animals and a greedy tortoise. The melodic rise and fall of his voice, the way he made her sigh one moment and gasp the next, was entrancing to witness.

Then, he saw her and the intensity of his lingering gaze set Freya's body on fire. Her hair was a tangle of wild curls, still dripping from the tub. Her nightgown molded to her wet skin. It didn't matter.

She stood still, unable to hear the words, feeling naked before him. She couldn't move. It was as if a chain were being forged between them, each link glowing red with heat she'd never experienced.

When the story was done and Ella stood up, Freya silently backed into the room and pulled a shawl around her. A moment later, her niece skipped in through the door with a happy smile. With a cheerful "good night," the cherub jumped into the bed.

As her eyes began to droop, Ella again murmured a few words about the benefits of choosing the captain as a husband over Colonel Richard. Freya wasn't the only one enthralled with Gregory Pennington, but she couldn't bring herself to remind the child that she had no choice.

When Ella dropped off to sleep, Freya's gaze moved to the door that stood slightly ajar. She wondered if Gregory was still out there. Gathering the shawl around her, she tiptoed over, intending to close it. At the last moment, she couldn't help but look. He was standing by the window, and his gaze immediately lifted to her.

His feet were bare. His shirt, hanging loose over his trousers, was only buttoned halfway. Freya never imagined she could find the state of a man's undress so exciting.

She supposed she owed him a word of thanks for making certain Ella didn't get into any mischief by escaping their bedchamber. Well, that was the fib Freya told herself as she padded into the sitting room, closing the door softly behind her.

Before she could say a word, Gregory strode across the room. His hand reached for hers and whatever she was going to say was lost forever. He never paused as their fingers entwined and he pulled her toward his bedchamber.

It was madness, but she didn't want it to stop.

He drew her through the door, leaving it slightly open and backing her against the wall.

"I want to kiss you," he whispered, his smoldering eyes meeting hers. "Tell me you don't want the same thing and...and I'll behave as I know I should."

Desire ripped through her, an intense primitive force that left her trembling.

A throb low in her belly started to spread. "I've never been kissed."

He caressed the side of her face, his thumb brushing the sensitive skin of her bottom lip. She was aware that her breaths were shallow and quick.

"Let me be your first." He came closer, his body was a whisper away from hers.

She should stop this, step away from him. She'd never been with any man, but she wasn't insensible to his meaning. Freya knew he was implying more. She tried desperately to think, but it was as if she'd fallen under a spell. All she could do was nod.

His lips touched hers, and all her worries disappeared in a whirlwind of awareness. He was gentle and patient, his firm lips softly playing with hers as if she were ripe fruit that he feared he might bruise. His fingers slid under the blanket of her hair and he caressed the sensitive skin of her neck. She melted into his touch and heard a soft cry of need spring from her lips.

Gregory deepened the kiss, his tongue teasing the seam of her lips. The throb in her belly became an ache, spreading through her limbs and to her breasts. Her lips parted under his, inviting him in, wanting, needing more of him. She heard his satisfied groan as his tongue slipped into her mouth.

The jolt of passion rushing through her buried the rest of her fears. In the next moment, Freya was kissing him back. Her hands stole around his neck, her tongue mimicking the dance she'd just learned.

Whatever shred of control he was hanging onto suddenly disappeared. His fingers curled into her hair and he pulled her head back, his mouth taking, drinking in what she was willingly offering him.

This man's body called to her. It was a mystery to be explored. She took her hands from around his neck and trailed her fingers over the linen of his shirt until they found their way inside. The hot skin scorched her. She felt the steely ridge of powerful shoulders and caressed the dusting of hair on his chest.

"You're driving me mad, Freya," he whispered against her lips before his hands slid down along her spine and cupped her bottom. He pressed her against his hardness and pushed a thigh between her legs until she gasped.

She was trapped, but there was nowhere else she wanted to be. The feel of her body against his was a miracle.

His lips left her mouth and moved over her face, dropping to her jaw. When they sank to the sensitive skin of her throat, she pressed her back more fully against the wall, willingly offering him her body. All of her.

Every nerve in her body cried for more when his fingers stroked her hard nipple through the nightgown and then tested the heavy fullness of her breast in his hand.

The pressure in her belly continued to build. She

couldn't think or focus. She was robbed of breath, but still she wanted more.

Bringing his mouth back to her lips, he whispered, "Ride me."

His voice was ragged, his breath as short as hers. She didn't know what he meant and then he pressed his leg against her sex. Her thighs clenched around his muscles, as she felt a wetness in her very center. Giving in to some primal instinct, she began to rock against him and he ran his fingers along the neckline of the nightgown, pushing it off her shoulders. She slipped her arms out, and it dropped to her waist as his mouth closed around a nipple.

She cried out softly, her fingers delving into his hair, her hands caressing his cheek while he suckled her. She wanted him never to stop. Stormy pressures were building within her. Seeing the dark planes of his face against her pale skin as his mouth moved to bring her pleasure was the most erotic thing she could ever have imagined possible.

She was barely aware of the moment when her world shifted. Wrapped around him, she came apart, burying her cries of release against his chest.

This was a first for him.

Holding Freya, wrapped around her body as she'd wrapped herself around his heart, Penn felt the pounding in his chest begin to diminish. Never in his life had he felt more protective of a woman than he felt about her right now. Never before had he wondered if this woman was the one with whom he was intended to spend his life.

She lifted her head off his shoulder and straightened

her nightgown, covering herself. He backed away and picked up the shawl from the floor. Even in the fading light of the fire, he saw the blush spreading across the fair skin of her chest and throat and cheeks. She avoided looking into his eyes.

"I...I am...I shouldn't have..." Her words trailed off.

He gently lifted her chin, meeting her dark gaze. "You and I have been circling each other from the moment we took to the road. Seeing you come out of that room, I forgot about right and wrong. I wanted you."

He brushed his lips against hers and was relieved to have her kiss him back, even though she withdrew again too quickly.

"I am the caretaker of a child," she said, flattening her palm against his chest as he moved to kiss her once more. "It would ruin everything for me and for Ella...here... being discovered."

She was right. He was glad one of them had enough sense to stop and think. Ella could be wandering in here at any moment. Shona and her husband were also close by. How difficult would it be for Freya if she were discovered in his bedroom?

With a feathery touch, she caressed his jaw and pressed a quick kiss to his chin before gathering the shawl tightly around herself and slipping out of his bedroom. A moment later, he heard the door to her room open and close.

Standing in his own doorway, Penn paused and recalled the vision of Freya standing outside of her bedchamber, watching them. The light brown hair, darkened with water from the bath, cascaded in waves of curls to her waist. Her eyes were wide and shining in the firelight. Her long white nightgown clung to her body, the wet cloth hugging her breasts and hips provocatively. How he'd ever continued with that story was a mystery, for looking at her there, he'd been a lost man.

The child had returned to Freya in their room after he was done with the fable, but he couldn't retire. Waiting in the sitting room, pacing from window to fireplace and back again, he'd brooded over the changes that had taken hold of him. He'd needed to touch her. Kiss her. Make her understand the effect she had on him. Sleep had been the furthest thing from his mind. But when she'd emerged once again and then had come willingly into his bedroom, he'd been able to only give her a glimpse of what could be between them.

Now, more than ever, he wanted to make love to her. The intensity of his desire was terrifying. Never before had he felt such hunger for a woman. But when she emerged once again and then come willingly into his bedroom, he'd been able to only give her a glimpse of what could be between them.

He turned and looked back at his bed. He wouldn't lure her into it. She had too much at stake. He wouldn't take advantage of her, not while in his own mind he was still trying to decide if she and Ella could be his future.

There was no question that any man who married Freya would find he'd won a prize to be cherished. But that meant settling down. Committing himself. Giving up his plans of moving to Boston and building the cities of that new nation.

Was he ready to rethink his entire future?

He had a great deal he needed to consider before they reached Baronsford.

✣   7   ✣

THOUGH THE HOUR was not late, the moon had already risen high in the starry sky by the time they reached Aberdeen and the home of Captain John Simpson and his very pregnant wife, Myrna.

When their carriage rolled to a stop outside the front door, the grey stone house seemed to Freya to sparkle in the moonlight, and every window was ablaze with a warm welcoming light. Her first impressions had not been wrong, either, for the delighted couple could not have been more hospitable in greeting and ushering them into their home.

Myrna, already exuding a maternal air as she moved gracefully through the rooms, was especially excited to spend time with Ella, who was also quite interested in their hostess. Together, the two played games and chatted while Freya settled in and prepared for dinner.

After the unexpected events in Gregory's bedchamber last night, she had felt awkwardly transparent in the carriage today and was relieved to have Ella's attention focused on someone else. As they'd ridden along past forests and farms, she could not look at Gregory and not recall the feel of his mouth on her lips and throat and breasts. Every time a rut or turn in the road caused their legs to touch, she again felt the pressure of those thighs that had made her fly apart with pleasure. She traveled the entire day in a perpetual state of excitement, and she felt as if Ella was far too aware of her agitation.

Passion. How was it that she'd reached her age and never known the overwhelming response it wrought in a person's body and mind? What Gregory made her feel last night had irrevocably changed her, and she'd experienced it without him ever taking her to his bed. He had satisfied needs in her that she barely knew existed. But what about his needs?

As they all sat together at dinner, Freya felt his gaze continue to come back to her, but she avoided looking at him. The infatuation she'd developed for Captain Pennington only added to the awkwardness she was feeling. But however she felt about him, she was fascinated to hear the story that John Simpson shared with them after Ella, allowed to dine with the adults at Myrna's insistence, asked about the man's limp.

"I don't mind talking about it at all," he said to the little girl. "I came away from battle with this limp, but if it weren't for this man's courage, I'd have certainly lost my life."

From the moment Captain Simpson raised his glass to Gregory, Ella wasn't the only one who was impatient to hear the story. Freya found herself hanging on his every word.

"It all happened at a place called Benavente in Spain," he told them. "We were both attached to Lord Paget's forces at the time, though we scarcely knew each other then. The army was moving west, trying to reach the sea. It was nine years ago this month, and the wintry weather was hard upon us. The ground was half frozen, and a river we'd just crossed was swollen from the recent rains. We engineers had just demolished the bridge, but the French cavalry crossed the river anyway. Perhaps eight hundred of them."

He paused and sipped his wine. Everyone at the table was focused on him, with the exception of Gregory, who was staring into his glass.

"The bullets were flying and the sabers were flashing," he continued, telling his story directly to Ella. "I took a bullet in this leg and went down in the middle of the battle. I thought I was finished, for the hooves of horses pounded about my head. Suddenly, I felt myself hoisted up from the ground and thrown over the shoulder of your gallant captain."

Simpson again raised his glass to Gregory.

"With his own sword swinging, he fought off the enemy as he carried me from the field to safety. Lord knows how far it was, but he never paused for breath before climbing onto a stray warhorse and galloping back into the fray. I earned a limp for my troubles, but I'd have died out there as sure as we're sitting here. And I have one man to thank for it, and that hero deserves and has my gratitude forever."

Their host sat back after finishing the story, and Freya and Ella looked as one to Gregory. He'd never mentioned any account of this bravery in all their talk about his past.

"Captain Simpson here has been known to embellish details a wee bit," he said, obviously uncomfortable with the looks of hero worship on the faces of the women at the table. He glared at his friend. "It'll be no time before you're saying that I descended from a cloud and parted the sea to save you."

A humble champion, Freya thought.

Ella knelt up on her seat and opened her arms to Gregory, who was seated beside her. "May I have a hug from a hero?"

Obviously surprised and moved by her request, he looked at Freya before hugging the child to his chest.

She brought her napkin to her lips to hide the sudden trembling of her chin. Affection for him permeated her very being. A bond had formed between Ella and the captain, one that she guessed her niece would always remember and look back on fondly.

Since they were finished with their meal, Freya excused herself and Ella, deciding this was the best time to tuck her niece in bed. Upstairs, as Shona joined them and pulled Ella's nightgown over the little one's head, the story they heard downstairs was retold with flourishes to the nursemaid. Settling Ella in the bed, Freya expected to hear more questions about the war, since she'd lost her father in it. And she was surprised to find that the direction of her niece's curiosity was focused on their hostess.

"Is Mrs. Simpson going to die after she has her baby?"

"No. No, sweetheart. Not all mothers die delivering their babies," Freya assured her, caressing the soft curls as Shona sat in a chair by the fire, working on her sewing.

"How many of them *do* die?"

"I don't know," she said, trying to think through what she was about to say, already knowing every answer would only trigger a dozen more questions. "Not too many."

"When you marry Captain Pennington and—"

"I am *not* marrying Captain Pennington," she

corrected, ignoring the snort coming from the area of the nursemaid.

"When you marry Captain Pennington," Ella started again.

Freya frowned at her niece.

"Very well," the child said. "When you marry *Gregory* and get big in the belly like Mrs. Simpson, will you promise me not to die?"

Simpson's cigar had gone out twice since the two men were left alone in the dining room, and Penn saw it was about to go out again. His friend was a man who focused on one thing when he warmed to a subject, and he was particularly enthused about this one.

"They've begun calling Union Street the 'Granite Mile' and it's a thing to behold. Putting in the street took tremendous skill, from an engineering perspective. We needed to level a good portion of St. Catherine's Hill and then build arches to carry the road over Putachieside. It's a thing of beauty, I swear to you."

John continued to elaborate on what had already been accomplished as well as the plans they had in the works. The changes were extensive, to be sure, but Penn knew the building here was not an isolated phenomenon. Major ports all over Scotland, including those in the Highlands, were undergoing expansion and improvement. Since the end of the French wars, shipbuilding and the fishing industries were becoming increasingly important, spurring the need for more and better harbor facilities, roads, and bridges. Men like Simpson and himself were needed to serve on civic building commissions in every major city. His skills would be in high demand if he were to stay in Scotland.

As his friend talked, however, Penn's mind drifted to Freya. The warm expression passing across her beautiful face when Ella called him a hero and hugged him was one that he could easily get used to.

"I need some information that you might have, John," he said when his friend had finished opening up most of the Highlands with hypothetical new macadam roads. "Tell me what you know about Colonel Richard Dunbar."

"He's a bad egg, as you know," Simpson responded, pouring more wine for the two of them. "A relation to your Miss Freya, isn't he?"

"A greedy relation. A cousin standing in the wings, waiting for her father to die. Dunbar becomes baron when he does and inherits a respectable fortune in the process." Penn made no mention of the fact that Freya intended to marry the scoundrel.

"Nothing new about that," Simpson observed. "But unless the baron's health is in dire straits, I believe the colonel may be in serious trouble."

"What have you heard?"

"It's money, of course, as it usually is with fools who let the gaming tables get the better of them." He took a moment to light his cigar. "Everyone at Fort William knows he's in debt and over his head. No polite London society parties or gentleman's clubs out there, as you know. But the gaming hells..." He shook his head. "I just recently heard that Dunbar was talking about selling his commission to pay his debts, but it's not nearly enough."

"I don't imagine those sharps out there are about to look kindly on a long-term note from him."

"Not likely."

"How much does he owe?" Penn asked.

"Only rumors, of course. But the last I heard, he owed seven thousand pounds," Simpson told him.

Penn let out a low whistle.

"You and I have seen more than a few gentlemen over the years lose their fortunes."

Unfortunately, that was the truth. For many, gambling was a habit they couldn't break out of. Men would wager on everything from cards and dice and horses to a race between two dung beetles.

"They become so desperate that whatever honor they have left is cast aside," Simpson continued. "Lying, cheating, fleeing the country. Irreparably ruining a family's reputation. Men do foolish things when they fall on times like this."

And when Dunbar's carcass landed in a ditch—and Penn was certain that he would, eventually—Freya and Ella's future would be ruined. He couldn't allow that to happen.

"Do you know anything about any imminent marriage to a Caithness heiress?"

"I heard it, and it's all a lie. He's done this before to buy himself time. Six months ago, there were rumors about an engagement to an earl's daughter from Yorkshire. Again, a lie. The colonel's situation is dire."

❧   8   ❧

TODAY WAS the first time these two women met, but Freya had no doubt that if they lived in the same town, they'd be frequent visitors to each other's home. After leaving her sleeping niece with Shona watching over, she joined her hostess in the drawing room.

Myrna was curious about how she came to be raising Ella, so Freya told her of the fate of the girl's parents. After having spent some time in Ella's company, she was also interested in knowing how difficult it had been to raise such a bright and precocious five-year-old with no husband.

"I wouldn't know the difference," Freya replied frankly. "Between my father and Shona and a household of people who dote on my niece, I believe we've been managing the responsibility...collectively."

Asked about this trip to Baronsford, Freya simply told her that this was the first opportunity for the child to meet her paternal grandmother. She saw no reason to share anything about the dowager's ultimatum or even

Colonel Dunbar. At the mention of Lady Dacre, however, Myrna found another topic that connected them.

"Ah, the families of the very rich," she sighed. "I hope Ella's grandmother is an exception to most, for I believe the wealthy are tutored in the strategies of being difficult. I pray that your visit with her will be pleasant and free of any trouble."

Her words caused Freya to look closer at her hostess. "Captain Simpson's family has been challenging?"

The young woman paused, building her courage to voice what troubled her.

"They have been," Myrna admitted. "But if I can speak in confidence, they were against our marriage."

"I'm so sorry," Freya told her. "I can't imagine that anyone who has met you could have any objection."

"They've never met me," she said, "because I am half Scot and half Irish, and my father is a clergyman. Here I am a year later, carrying a child, and they still refuse to invite us to Staffordshire or acknowledge me in any way."

"I think that is unconscionable behavior on their part," Freya exclaimed, her heart going out to the young woman. Her sister had never met her husband's family, either. They'd shown no interest in seeing Ella.

Myrna managed a weak smile. "But none of that truly matters. John is the finest of husbands and terribly good at what he does. And as you see, we've established a home that we can be proud of."

Freya reached over and squeezed her friend's hand. "A home that soon will be bubbling with the laughter of your bairn."

Myrna's face bloomed. They were happy, regardless of family.

"So tell me about Captain Pennington," her host said,

changing the topic. "From what I saw tonight, the two of you have an understanding? Has he declared himself publicly?"

Freya felt her face immediately flush hot. She searched for an explanation to defuse any mistaken impression. "No! The captain and I are only friends. Ella's grandmother is meeting us at his family's home in the Borders because the Earl of Aytoun's estate in Hertfordshire is quite close to Lady Dacre's. It was only because of the captain's kindness and consideration that he is escorting us. If Ella's attachment to him has given you...she's so keen on...I don't..."

Myrna's hand softly touched Freya's, putting an end to the senseless babbling.

"I understand," the young mother-to-be said consolingly.

Efforts at denial continued to race through her mind, but after last night, it was all a lie. Something had certainly happened between them. Something wonderful and magical. She was a different woman today than the innocent who'd set out on this journey.

"Considering Captain Pennington's plans, I certainly understand your heartache."

A chasm opened beneath Freya, and hope drained out of her. A painful knot formed in her chest.

"Yes...his plans," she said, pretending that she was aware of whatever Myrna was referring to.

"When John heard the captain had notified the corps that he intended to resign his commission, he was happy for him until he heard he was planning on going to America." Myrna shook her head. "Boston is so far away."

"Boston," Freya repeated, her heart sinking even further.

"John says the captain has family there. An uncle and cousins. We understand Boston is a growing city where a man can make his mark, but it's not exactly home, is it?"

Boston. Feeling her chin begin to tremble, she stood, using the excuse of fetching a shawl from a chair across the room to buy herself a moment.

What was she thinking? she asked herself. How could she have been so foolish as to think their little romance on the road could magically resolve all of her troubles?

Picking up the shawl, she closed her eyes for a moment and thought of him. Gregory had never lied to her. He'd said a great deal about his past, but nothing about his plans for the future. Last night had been a gift. How else could she think of it?

"You didn't know, did you?"

Myrna's troubled tone made Freya turn around.

"I did. Of course," she lied. "As I said before, there is no understanding between me and Captain Pennington. None whatsoever."

As Penn and his host joined the women in the drawing room, his eyes immediately found Freya. He needed to steal her away. He had so much that he wanted to speak to her about—thoughts that were half-formed but that he still desired to share.

Two brightly upholstered settees faced each other by the fire, and she was sitting beside Myrna like an old friend. Her gaze fixed on him the moment they entered, her eyes caressing his face as if trying to lock his image in her memory. Or was it last night that she was thinking about? He didn't know.

Each time he saw her, he became more enraptured. With the firelight behind her, her light brown hair formed a halo around her angelic face. The desire to cross the room and take her into his arms was almost overpowering.

Their hostess rose and stretched a hand out to her husband. "Walk with me. Your child is being especially acrobatic tonight."

As the couple took their turns about the room, Penn moved to Freya, his leg brushing against her skirts as he sat beside her. He knew it was not his imagination when her shoulder pressed ever so gently against him. He took her hand in his and caressed the soft skin and slender fingers. John and his wife were on the other side of the room, their attention focused on each other. But if they were aware of their guests' conduct or not, Penn didn't care.

"I'm afraid I tire very easily these days," Myrna said, approaching them. "Please forgive my leaving you, but I must go up for the night."

Penn and Freya stood to say good night. Behind them, the fire popped and flared in the hearth, mirroring the tumult in his chest.

"If you'll excuse me, I'll be back down shortly," John said, adding, "I don't like her trying to manage those stairs by herself."

The moment the door closed behind their hosts, Penn took Freya in his arms. "I hoped to have this chance to tell you—"

He never finished for she raised her fingers to his lips.

"Thank you," she said softly. "Thank you for what you've done for Ella...and for me. Thank you for your generosity and your kindness. Thank you for accompanying us on this trip and giving us an experience that we'll cherish for—"

This time he was the one to interrupt. He kissed her, deeply. All the passion that had been building inside of him this entire day poured out like a torrent. A dam within him had burst, and he knew it.

The moment she leaned into his touch, he took possession of her mouth. He didn't let her go until he felt every layer of reserve drop away. She was kissing him back with as much fervor as he was feeling until he finally broke off the kiss. He had so much he wanted to say to her.

"I don't want gratitude. It is I who could go eternally about the change you have brought into my life." He could not contain the raging flood of emotions. "You and Ella are precious gems. Remember that. You cannot give yourself over to an uncertain...or unfavorable future."

She kissed him again. Her arms slid upward, encircling his neck. Her breasts pressed against him, and she placed soft kisses against his chin, on his lips. She ran her fingers through his hair, her mouth moving to his ear, where she tasted his earlobe.

"I don't want to talk of the future," she whispered. "Right now, I only want to feel and savor the stolen gift our time together has been. I want to treasure these precious moments."

Her words pushed all rational thought from his mind. Every day, they'd sat for hours across from each other in the carriage, wasting moments. How many times, today alone, had he fantasized about doing just this—feeling her body against his, feeling her lips against his?

She raised her mouth to be kissed again, and he took what she offered. His hand slid over her breast, touching her through the dress, kneading her firm flesh. She leaned into him, a soft moan escaping her.

Freya tore her mouth free. Her eyes were large and beautiful and filled with raw emotion when they looked into his. The burning color in her cheeks reflected the fire raging within her. And he wanted to be the wind that fanned those flames.

"I have stored up memories of being with you," she said raggedly. "They will be like flowers pressed into a sacred book. As the years pass, I shall page through these days and lift those faded blossoms to my lips, and remember. Right or wrong, I'll cherish the taste of passion you've shown me...long after I marry another."

After I marry another...

These stolen moments meant nothing without the promise of forever. The dazzling realization came to him with the unleashed power of a summer storm.

He was falling in love with her.

And he refused to imagine his life without her.

But he didn't have a chance to say the words, for a knock sounded and they jumped apart. Freya moved to stand in front of the fire, and their host entered.

❧   *9*   ☙

THE INN WAS a large stone building in Seagate, a bustling section of Dundee that was alive with activity. On the outskirts of the port, Freya watched as Gregory directed Ella's attention toward a curious hill rising above the town. The "Law" was known to be an ancient fairy fortress, he told her. From that moment on, the child's nose had been pasted to the window as they crawled through narrow streets jammed with carts and vendors. Down the smoky lanes, she excitedly pointed out the harbor with its forest of ships' masts, silhouetted by the rising moon. In the little girl's eyes, Dundee was far more impressive than any of the places they'd stopped before tonight.

Following the routine established during their journey, as soon as their luggage was carried up to the rooms the captain arranged for, Dougal left on his mission of searching for any sign of Colonel Dunbar.

They still had Stirling and Edinburgh to pass through before they reached Baronsford, but Freya sensed her cousin would find them here. Several of the colonel's letters had mentioned Dundee, a place he apparently visited often.

Since Aberdeen, Freya's mind had been wallowing in the dark inevitability of her future, and she'd spent the day trying to hide her unhappiness. But every time she spoke, her words sounded hollow.

Freya watched Ella flit like a bird in and out of the large, airy sitting room, exploring the three bedchambers. The inn's rooms here in Dundee were similar to those at Huntly, but larger and more comfortable. While Ella roamed, Freya and Shona reorganized the clothing in the trunks. In three days, she thought gloomily, they'd be meeting Lady Dacre. She wanted to be sure they were ready.

The little girl wandered across the sitting room and pulled a chair up to a window. Climbing up on it, she pressed her nose to the glass and peered down at the street.

"Where is he going?" Ella asked a moment later. "Is he abandoning us?"

The note of distress drew Freya's focus from her own misery.

Shona took a step over to the child and looked out the window. "Captain Pennington did just climb into the carriage, mistress. He's going off somewhere."

"He is probably visiting some friends." Freya kept her voice calm. "Or he has business to attend to."

Ella jumped off the chair and ran to her. "When is he coming back?"

"I don't know, my love."

"Isn't he going to have dinner with us? He still owes me a game of backgammon," she said, tugging on Freya's hand. "How am I to go to sleep tonight unless he tells me another African story?"

Her own heartache was only compounded by Ella's obvious disappointment. Separating from him was going to be much, much harder than she imagined. For both her and Ella.

"I can tell you a story."

"No, I want the captain to do it."

She crouched down before her niece. "The captain is not ours to keep. He has other friends. People with whom he might like to spend time. We have to respect his privacy. We can't be expecting him to spend every minute with us."

"He doesn't spend every minute with us," Ella corrected her. "He sleeps in his own bed. That's not every minute."

Freya took a deep breath, trying to keep her own emotions in check.

"I think it's time, sweetheart, for us to loosen our grip on Captain Pennington," she said gently. "And it would be better to do it now, rather than later. We have to allow him to live his own life too."

Ella shook her head. "He likes us. I know it. He likes to be with us. He looks at you all day long."

"He doesn't."

"He does too." Ella appealed to the nursemaid. "Tell her, Shona."

He does. He doesn't. He does. He doesn't. Freya wasn't about to play that game. She also wasn't about to involve Shona as an arbitrator. None of it made any difference. Gregory was going away.

"He can like us and still have his other friends too," she said, hoping this was a way to put an end to the conversation. "And if we like him anywhere near as much as he likes us, then we have to allow him to go."

"Allow him to go where?"

"Anywhere he wants to."

"Where?" Ella wouldn't give up.

"I don't know, my love. Baronsford. London. Boston. Wherever he wants to go."

"Where is Boston?"

"It's across the sea, in America."

"America?" Ella cried out, her chin beginning to quiver. "But that's too far away!"

Freya agreed, but what could she do about it? What difference did it make that she was starting to love him? She knew he cared for her and for Ella, but he had dreams of his own to pursue. Dreams that took him far from the Highlands, far from Scotland. Their paths had crossed for only this moment in time, and it had changed her, given her something special that she would cherish forever, but he could not give her a future they could share. And she would never ask it of him. She would never try to hold him. What kind of love would require the sacrifice of a dream?

Reaching out, she pulled her niece into her embrace. But before she could console her further, a knock drew their attention to the door.

Shona answered it and Dougal stepped in.

"He's here, mistress. Captain Dunbar. He's found us. Downstairs, he is."

———

Colonel Dunbar was waiting for her in a private dining room off the inn's taproom.

In the eighteen months since she'd last seen him, the changes in her cousin's features were marked. When he stood to greet her with a bow, his manner still conveyed the self-assurance of a man convinced he could charm the feathers off a peacock. But the sallow complexion with the ruddy blotches on his puffy cheeks and nose told her this was a man often in his cups, a condition she'd always suspected. His bloodshot eyes were still shrewd, however, and he gazed at her appraisingly as she declined the chair the waiter held for her.

As he dismissed the waiter, the thought struck her that this man was the reality of her future life. He was a small man. A head shorter than Gregory, at least. The careless air he attempted to convey was belied by the constant and rapid movement of his gaze, as well as the nervous tic on the right side of his face. Standing eye-to-eye with him, she struggled to hide her disappointment. Colonel Richard Dunbar did not measure up to Gregory Pennington. Not even close. But then again, no one measured up to Gregory Pennington.

"My apologies for not meeting you earlier," he said. "It was difficult to break away from my duties."

"I'm relieved that you caught up to us here," she said politely, trying to keep any note of emotion out of her tone. "We've had a comfortable journey so far, thanks to the Pennington family, and as it stands, we should arrive at Baronsford with a few days to spare."

She again shook her head at the offer of a seat.

"As I mentioned in my letter," she continued, "I'll be introducing you to Lady Dacre as my intended, and—"

"About that," he interrupted. "Our plans have changed."

For an insane moment, she wondered if the rumors

Gregory had told her were the truth. Could it be that he was already married? But she had no time to either celebrate or mourn such an event.

"I've decided that we shall arrive at Baronsford *already* married."

Freya's heart sank. "Already married?"

"Yes," he responded flatly, brushing at a speck on the cuff of his uniform. "There is a solicitor here in Dundee that I have had business dealings with in the past. We shall stand before him tomorrow, exchange our oaths, and sign a contract of marriage. This way, Lady Dacre will have no doubts about your niece's future."

Freya's mind raced. She was no fool. She'd known this man her entire life. He was not one to do anything for anyone unless he benefited somehow.

"There's no need for such a drastic step," she said.

"Do you really consider it 'drastic', Miss Freya?" he asked with a feigned air of nonchalance.

"What I mean is that I believe Lady Dacre would be satisfied meeting you and knowing of our engagement," she told him. "I see no need to delay an extra day here."

"You just said yourself that we're ahead of schedule," he said. He shrugged and then fixed his shrewd eyes on her. "But it doesn't matter. I insist that the wedding take place here, before we get one step closer to Baronsford."

There was no point in arguing about waiting for a church wedding. They both knew that in Scotland, the exchange of marriage vows did not require the authority of a church to make the union legal. No reading of banns was needed, only a witness to attest that the couple declared themselves married before him. Her sister's marriage had not taken place in a church. But Lucy and Fredrick Dacre had been in love.

Freya looked on at her cousin's cold expression.

"Why?" she asked. "Why are you so adamant about this wedding taking place *now*?"

"Isn't it what you want?" he replied. "Marriage? Security for your precious niece?"

She wasn't satisfied with his refusal to answer.

"What is the *reason* for this haste?" she persisted. "You know that my fortune is modest. You'll eventually inherit the Sutherland estates." Freya paused as the light dawned.

Dunbar wouldn't say the words but the truth was too obvious.

"You need my five thousand pounds now. As my husband, you take that money for yourself."

"Very well," he said with a toss of his head. "What of that? We both need something right now. You need a husband—or the promise of one—to keep your niece. I need money for...well, what I need it for is my affair. We each get what we bargained for."

He pulled a card from his hat and flipped it onto the table next to her.

"You'll find the address of the solicitor on his card. I expect you to be there tomorrow at nine o'clock...sharp."

Freya stared at the card as he walked past her. She was no gambler, but she knew he was holding the winning hand. She had no choice but to show up tomorrow and marry the man.

The bells in a half dozen of Dundee's church towers were ringing out eight o'clock as Penn climbed from the carriage in front of the inn. The streets of Seagate were still alive and active, but sailors and dockworkers intent on revelry had now replaced the day's carters and vendors. Climbing the stairs to their rooms, he was happy to realize that it was early enough. Freya would still be awake. They had so much they needed to discuss.

He found the sitting room empty and frowned in the direction of Freya's closed door. Ella would undoubtedly be asleep by now, and he wondered how he could get Freya to come out without disturbing the child. His dilemma was resolved before he had time to hang his greatcoat.

The door creaked open. The problem was that Ella was the one who slipped out.

"Not asleep yet, eh?" he asked softly, watching the child close the door quietly. "Where is your aunt?"

Ella put a finger to her lips and tiptoed away from the door. "She cried herself to sleep."

Ordinarily, Penn would have considered her words part and parcel with her usual dramatics. But there was a difference in her tone...and in the red-rimmed eyes. She walked slowly toward him, her trembling chin on her chest, her eyes avoiding contact.

"Hullo there, what's wrong?" He crouched down on one knee.

She stopped just out of his reach. "Why do you have to go to Boston?"

"Boston?" he asked. How the blazes did she know about Boston?

The Simpsons, he realized. Freya must have learned about it from Myrna.

"Is that why she's crying?" he asked gently, glancing over at the closed door.

"Her life is a ruin. But she's being a martyr." A tear

streaked down the child's cheek and she stabbed at it. "*He's* here and she's going to marry him. Tomorrow."

The low-down conniver! The calculating scoundrel!

He took hold of Ella's shoulders and looked into her face. This was the first time he'd seen her shed actual tears. "Colonel Dunbar came *here?*"

"Fie went downstairs to speak with him," Ella said, sniffling. "She was crying when she came back up. Fie never cries. I heard her tell Shona to keep me here tomorrow morning until she signed the papers and came back."

Blast him, Penn thought. He should have known Dunbar would catch up to them here. Why couldn't the rogue show up in Stirling? Or Edinburgh? He thought he'd be prepared for it.

He wasn't, however, and this news of Dunbar's meeting with Freya chilled him.

Penn drew Ella to his chest and pressed a kiss onto her hair. "I want you to go back to bed, little one."

"But I can't sleep. I'm mourning."

"You shouldn't mourn. You go back to bed, and I promise to take care of things."

"How will you take care of things?" she wanted to know.

"It will be a surprise."

The little girl's face lifted, the brown eyes rounding with hope. "I like surprises."

"Excellent. Then, off to bed with you."

Ella started to go and then stopped. "I have one question."

"What is it?"

"What *is* mourning?"

The waiter downstairs had been a little hesitant about helping Penn, but a little monetary incentive had loosened his tongue. The colonel had asked if the Mermaid, a gaming den, was still shut down. Learning it was open again—for the time being—he'd gone off.

The Mermaid turned out to be a rat's nest, located on the ground floor of a dilapidated building down by the docks. Whores and drunks milled about in front of the place, which was distinguished by a pair of thugs standing beneath a green lantern.

The two bruisers gave him a looking over and then one jerked a thumb, which Penn took as permission to go in. Reminding himself to keep his focus on the business side of what he had to do, he pushed open the heavily scarred door, ducked his head, and entered the stinking, smoke-filled rooms.

During their days on the road, Penn had gotten the idea that Freya thought a mere introduction of the colonel to Lady Dacre would be enough. Perhaps that was all the dowager required. But after what Penn had heard from John Simpson, he knew that a promise of future liquidity was not sufficient for Dunbar. The colonel needed access to money that was available now, and he wanted it fast. Every sharp in Scotland had muscle like the two out front, and they loved extracting payments from debtors. Particularly from gentlemen.

Searching through the crowded rooms, Penn knew he was gambling, as well. He was acting on behalf of Freya while she was still unaware of his intentions. They had not declared their affection. It was possible that he was off in his assumption that she didn't want to marry

Dunbar. And what about her father's feelings about Dunbar as a son-in-law? That aspect of the situation had never even been hinted at.

Perhaps it was a gamble, but Penn liked his odds.

For the first time in his life, he was acting on the emotional impulses of his heart instead of the rational processes of his mind. As he spotted Dunbar at a card table in a private room at the very back of the place, Penn hoped he was doing the right thing.

He walked toward his rival, and the colonel eyed him steadily, appraising him. Friend? Agent of the general's staff? Another card player that he could take advantage of? From the scarcity of coins in front of him, Dunbar appeared to be losing.

"I'm Captain Pennington, Colonel," he said, clearing away any confusion as he arrived at the table.

Recognition was immediate. "I'm grateful for all you've done for Miss Freya on this journey, Pennington." Dunbar made a motion to an open seat at the table. "Would you care to join us for a drink and perhaps some cards?"

Penn shook his head. "I need a private moment with you. Now, if you don't mind."

There was a long pause as they stared at each other. Penn wasn't asking. He was telling him.

He had never possessed a quick temper, like his father, the Earl of Aytoun, or his brother, Viscount Greysteil. He'd never called out another man to fight a duel. In public argument, he tended to be the voice of reason. But right now, looking at Dunbar, the irritation that was building in him made him consider lifting the man physically out of that chair.

A gambler survives by reading the face and physical

movement and attitude of his opponent. The colonel must have read the danger he was facing.

"Would you two gentlemen be so kind as to have a drink at the bar," Dunbar said to the other card players, never taking his eyes off Penn. "On me, of course, while I speak with the good captain. Then we'll pick up our game where we left off. Shall we?"

When the room was left to them, Penn sat and started in directly.

"Seven thousand pounds."

The colonel stared at him, the scant color in his face draining away.

"I see the number rings a bell with you."

"What can I do for you, Captain?"

Penn reached into his jacket and produced a folded paper, setting it on the table.

"You have a fortnight to come up with two thousand pounds to pay Whitey Boyd at Oban, who's been known to gut men for less. And another thousand to Everett Read at Inverness in a month, and I hear he's already put out the word he'll have your head. And worst of all, you're overdue with the four thousand you owe Jack MacDonald at Leith, who for all we know is waiting outside for you."

"What do *you* want?"

"I want to give you your life back. I want to give you that money."

Dunbar's mouth opened as if he were about to speak, but he said nothing. He simply stared uncomprehendingly at Penn, who slid the paper across the table.

"I want to make a deal."

Dunbar read the document, and Penn waited until understanding lit the unhealthy features. He pushed the paper away.

"You want me to give up Torrishbrae for a worthless title and nothing else," he complained.

"And seven thousand pounds."

"I barely come out even, if I sign this."

Penn slid a bank draft for seven thousand pounds across the table.

Dunbar's eyes grew wide at the sight of it.

"And since I feel particularly generous today..." He took a second bank draft from his jacket. "This will be in return for signing the contract now. And that brings the total to ten thousand. Would that suit you?"

☙   10   ❧

Freya wanted to be on her way before Ella stirred.

Shona knew what was to be done, and the nursemaid was waiting in the sitting room when Freya tiptoed out of the bedchamber.

"What should I tell him when he asks?" Shona asked.

Freya cast a longing look at Gregory's door as she fetched her greatcoat. "Tell him you don't know where I went. Tell him I'll explain when I return."

"Won't it be too late by then?"

Freya pulled on her coat and buttoned it. Too late for what? Too late to play on the conscience of a genuinely good man? Too late to make him change his plans and turn his life upside down? Too late to be rescued from a dismal future?

In her heart, she knew it was already too late. Nothing could change what she needed to do. She loved Gregory, and *because* of that, she would do nothing to interfere with the path in life he'd chosen. It was true that she'd altered her path for her sister five years ago. But she'd been rewarded with Ella. A child that she could not love more if she herself had given birth to her.

After asking directions, Freya set off on foot toward the legal district on High Street.

The December wind whipped her blue greatcoat about her with savage fury. Freya forced herself to push aside the yearning of her heart. She needed to focus on the nuptials that were about to take place. She was not the first woman to enter into a loveless union. Hardly, she chided herself. And she had good reason for doing it. By all the stars in heaven, she would smile and lie and appear satisfied in the eyes of Lady Dacre. She would do whatever needed to be done to keep Ella safe with her.

But the unknown future was what continued to tear at her now.

She feared what her cousin would do to Torrishbrae and the people who depended on her. What if he were to assert his rights as husband and demand that she leave the Highlands? Her father depended on her to run the estate. The colonel had no attachment to the land. Once he had control of it, she had no doubt he would run it into the ground to satisfy those men he owed money to. Casting about desperately in her mind for solutions, she thought that perhaps there was a chance of negotiating with the man or with the men her cousin was indebted to. Perhaps...

Her thoughts ground to a halt as she realized she was passing by the distinctive town building known as the Pillars. Two doors farther down she stopped at her destination.

She had to go in, but she couldn't get her feet to move. The bell in a nearby clock tower struck nine, rousing her. Finally, with an act of sheer will, she dragged herself to the door of the building. Thinking of why she was doing this, she wrapped the iron fist of reason around her bleeding heart, squeezing into submission all romantic notions, all dreams, all hopes.

A passing clerk inside directed her up the stairs to the chambers occupied by the colonel's solicitor.

The stairwell was dark and airless, it seemed, like a passage in an ancient crypt. With every anguished step she took, her time with Gregory appeared before her. The words they'd spoken danced in her mind. The memories of those stolen moments of passion—moments that she thought would keep her sane in the years to come—now threatened to choke her and drive her mad.

Finally, Freya found herself standing at the fateful door, summoning the strength to knock. Her chin trembled as the vision of Gregory and Ella sitting together by the fire emerged from the dark oak panel of the door. She saw the child cuddled against him, the look of wonder on her face as he entertained her with his stories. She recalled the patience he displayed whenever her niece was too tired and misbehaved. She thought of them all skating on the ice.

What kind of relationship did Dunbar have with Ella? Twice, the colonel had come to Torrishbrae in the past five years, and each time he'd kept his distance from the 'troublesome noise', as he'd referred to her.

Tears burned a path down her face.

The realization was as sudden and certain as death. It was impossible. She might as well try to live without breathing. She couldn't do it, not like this, not under Dunbar's conditions as they were. There was far more than her own future at stake. Ella's. Her father's. The tenants at Torrishbrae.

She turned and hurried to the stairs. As she began to descend, the solicitor's door swung open.

"Freya?"

Gregory's voice made her clutch at the wall. She stopped and looked back at him. Light poured into the dark passage from behind him, and his tall frame filled the doorway.

He stepped toward her. "I've been waiting for you."

She stared in confusion at his outstretched hand, listening to the drumming of her heart. She was dreaming. She was imagining all of this. This couldn't be Gregory, she told herself. He was back at the inn...with Ella and Shona.

He came down the few steps and wrapped an arm around her. "Will you come in with me?"

She blinked, allowing her gaze to move over his lips. She stared into the eyes that had enthralled her the moment she'd first looked into them.

Was Dunbar already there? she wondered vaguely.

Chaos reigned in her mind. How could Gregory also be there? Feeling as if she'd been struck by lightning, she allowed him to lead her back to the door.

Before they went in, he ran his thumb over the wetness on her cheeks and then brushed his lips against hers.

"I'm sorry you've had a shock, but I had a great deal to do this morning."

"This morning?" she managed to murmur.

"I'd like you to come in and listen to what the solicitor has to say. Can you do it?"

"The colonel's solicitor?"

"No. Mine."

She felt herself being swept up on a wave of hope. "Why would your solicitor be here?"

"Just come in and sit down...and trust me."

As his man Oliver Ogilvie explained what Colonel Dunbar had agreed to, Penn held Freya's trembling fingers in his and watched her profile as she recognized the impact this change would have on her future. She glanced at Penn for a moment as the solicitor laid the signed documents out before her.

"Although Colonel Dunbar will inherit the title of 'baron' after your father's demise, he surrenders any future claim to Torrishbrae and its associated Sutherland land and property," the solicitor summarized. "And, as is stated on the last page, he abandons any offers of marriage and releases you of any 'understandings' between the two of you. You are free, Miss Sutherland, to plan your future as you please."

By now, Penn thought, Dunbar would be halfway to Edinburgh to cash the bank drafts he'd received in exchange for signing the document, and Freya was free to stand in front of Lady Dacre as a wealthy and independent woman. She was free to forge a future of her own. In any court of law, she could fight for the custody of her niece, for she now had the means to provide a secure future for Ella, even after her father was gone.

"If you have no questions for me..." the solicitor stated, rising from his chair. He turned to Penn and said, "I'll be in the adjoining chamber, Captain, if my services are needed again."

Freya waited until the man had left the room before standing and turning her teary eyes on him.

"How much did this cost you, Gregory? How am I ever going to be able to repay you?"

He rose to his feet and wrapped her in his arms. "I only ask you to answer one question."

Penn could see his face reflected in the dark jewels of her eyes.

"From the first moment I laid eyes on you, I found that I could not ignore my feelings. I could not ignore the changes I felt taking place in me. Day after day, my admiration grew, and with it my affection. And it wasn't only your beauty that I fell in love with...it was your generous and selfless heart."

He kissed her lips and drew back, looking steadily into that face he knew he could never again live without.

"I love you, Freya."

She stood still, unsure of the reality of this moment, caught up in a storm of joy so strong that she felt herself going weak in the knees. Afraid to hope, afraid to let herself believe, she stared up at him.

"Please tell me this is not all a dream."

He smiled and held her tight. "If it is, the good news is that we're dreaming together."

Her vision misted over. "Then since we're together—awake or dreaming—I should tell you that I love you too. But dreams are such fleeting things. And you have plans."

A broad smile spread across his face. "We're not asleep, my love, though this world is still our own. And I want you to know that I am *not* going off to Boston. That was a plan made by a man who was looking for a purpose in his life. A man who needed to establish a home and create a family. In you, I have already found both. If you'll have me."

Her palms flattened against his chest. Beneath her fingertips, she felt the strong beat of his true heart.

"Will you marry me, Freya?"

"But your family. Our stations in life are so different," she cried. "I promised myself long ago that I would never be put in the same position my sister and Fredrick faced, what your friends John and Myrna have faced."

"You won't," he interrupted, wiping the tears off her cheek. "My parents, my brother and sisters—they're nothing like Dacre's family. I guarantee you that they will embrace you and Ella as their own."

She started to argue, and he pressed a finger to her lips.

"You can trust me, Freya. After all, the Penningtons are half Scot. They'll love you as I love you. Say you'll marry me."

Emotions choked the words in her throat. All she could do was nod.

He kissed her, deeply and passionately.

"I don't want you to think I was taking you for grant-ed," he said as they broke off the kiss. "But I took a chance and had Ogilvie draw up the marriage contract."

"For us?" she asked. Love and happiness welled up within her until she thought she would burst.

He nodded. "So what would you think about two weddings? One here, now, and the second in a church where your family and mine can share in our joy?"

Exchanging their vows was bliss. Signing and swearing the oath before Mr. Ogilvie was simple. Consummation, however, was certain to present a few difficulties. At the top of that list was a little girl named Ella.

Between breathless kisses during the carriage ride back to the inn, Freya learned that her niece had met with Gregory last night and told him about the arrival of Dunbar. Now, as the two sat hand in hand in the sitting room, sharing their news with the five-year-old, Ella first bounced with joy and then took immediate credit for it all.

Then the inquisition began.

"Are you married like Captain Simpson and Mrs. Simpson?" her niece wanted to know.

"We are indeed," Gregory answered.

She addressed the next question to Freya. "Are you married like Shona and Dougal?"

"Yes."

Ella made a face, as if she might not be too keen on that arrangement. "Am I allowed to come to your bedchamber when you are in bed?"

"No," she said.

"But if you knock," Gregory explained, "one of us will fetch you. But not until we're ready for you."

"Why?"

"Because it would be inappropriate," Freya told her. "A husband and wife need their privacy."

"Why?"

Freya didn't recall her niece being as curious about Shona and her husband. "Sometimes we need to...talk. Just the two of us."

"I'll cover my ears when I come in." She covered her ears with her hands, showing them how she'd do it.

"Still, you need to knock," Freya reminded her. "And wait."

Ella pulled her legs up and sat cross-legged on her chair. She was settling in for the long haul. "Only talk? How about dancing?"

Gregory sent Freya a troubled look, and she was sure he was remembering the day Ella became upset in the carriage, thinking that dancing was responsible for making babies. She looked at her niece.

"We'll be dancing too," she said softly. Ella's gaze immediately fixed on Freya's stomach. "But I'll be fine, my love. I won't leave you."

The child's expression bespoke her doubts, and Freya lifted the girl onto her lap.

Holding Ella tight in her arms, she whispered, "I love you. We'll *never* leave you. You're going to be ours."

Satisfied, Ella extricated herself and dived into Gregory's arms. Freya watched, somewhat misty-eyed, as the little hands cradled his face and she looked into his eyes.

"What do I call you now?" she asked.

"Penn? Papa? Gregory? Uncle? Anything you like," he said gently.

Ella nodded thoughtfully, placed a kiss on his forehead, and then pointed to her own forehead. Gregory returned it with a smile. Kisses were then exchanged on each cheek before she scrambled to get down.

Standing in front of them, she looked from one to the other.

"Fie and Gag," she said.

"I like it," Gregory said, pulling Freya against him.

RULES ARE RULES, but making love while traveling with a five-year-old bent on getting one's attention at the worst time was proving to be a challenge. After an extra day in Dundee and two days in Stirling, Ella was continuing to burst into their room at the most unexpected moment. A stomach ache. A bad dream. Shona's loud snoring. And last night, she claimed she was starving and couldn't possibly go to sleep.

The first night, Shona had kept Ella away for at least half the night. Since then, Freya and Gregory found themselves making love anytime and anywhere the opportunity presented itself, stealing moments that were exciting, fiery, and tremendously satisfying.

In the carriage on the way to the top of Dundee Law while Ella taught Dougal to play backgammon back at the inn. Against an ancient wardrobe in their bedchamber while Shona bathed the child by the fire in the sitting room. In Stirling, where Gregory knew an old friend who was stationed at the snow-covered castle, they'd made love in his private office while the major showed Ella, with Shona trailing along, the gardens of the former royal residence. Freya still blushed at the memory of the ecstasy she and Gregory shared on the man's desk.

Freya's gaze lifted from her book to her husband. He was sitting with Ella across the drawing room of the Pennington's lovely townhouse in Edinburgh. The two had their heads together, whispering quietly and sending her occasional looks of mischief.

She loved them and she loved seeing the bond that had formed between them. Freya was especially appreciative of Gregory's understanding and patience regarding Ella's nightly interruptions. He understood that while they were on the road and away from her regular routines at home, the child needed attention.

Shona looked up from her sewing and cocked an eyebrow in the direction of her charge. It was past Ella's bedtime.

Freya started to remind her niece of it, but paused with surprise when the little girl hugged Gregory and then crossed the room to give her a goodnight hug too.

"I'm relying on you, Fie," she said. Taking Shona by the hand, Ella led her nursemaid out of the drawing room and up the stairs.

Relying on me? She gazed after her niece, wondering about the girl's happy disposition.

A few moments later, Gregory rose to his feet, and the smile he gave her tightened her chest with the love she held in her heart. She didn't think she would ever get used to how handsome he was or how breathless she felt when he looked at her like that.

"What does she mean, 'relying' on me?" she asked as

he strolled lazily across the room. He took the book out of her hand, laid it aside, and pulled her to her feet.

"Come on," he said, threading his fingers into hers and leading her up the stairs to their bedroom.

This was how every night started, but a few moments after their door closed, Ella would be there, demanding their attention.

Freya heard the door close, and she looked over her shoulder as Gregory moved behind her to undo the buttons of her dress.

"How long do you think we have?" she asked.

She shivered with excitement as his lips brushed against the side of her neck.

"We have all night."

She didn't want to ruin the magic of this moment by reminding him of the past few nights. Instead, Freya gathered her hair to one side as Gregory's strong fingers undid and parted the dress on her back.

He pushed the dress down over her arms, and she looked nervously at the door. "Do you think we should put a chair in front of it?"

The child was definitely confused as far as what was considered appropriate knocking at their door. Last night, there was a soft tap, and then she'd put a shoulder to it.

"Maybe that desk," she suggested next. "The two of us should be able to move it over."

Still worrying about how Ella would manage to gain access to their room, Freya heard him chuckle to himself, but she was momentarily distracted by the feel of his fingers moving over her body.

"The window," she said warily, taking a step toward it. "Isn't that a balcony outside? We should check to see if she can reach..."

Her words disappeared when he turned her around and she found he was standing naked in front of her. *Naked.* She raked his body with her gaze.

"When did you undress me?" she asked, realizing they were both as naked as the day they were born. Shyness quickly gave way to excitement, and desire lit up within her like a flame.

"You are stunning," he said, his voice husky with feeling.

Her body hummed as he stroked his fingers over her breasts and belly before he bent down and drew her nipple between his lips.

She sighed with pleasure, her head falling back. "Please build a fortress and make sure no one interrupts us at least for an hour," she moaned.

"We have all night," he repeated, suckling hard at her other breast.

His hand slid down over her mound and into her waiting sex. Freya inhaled sharply and her fingers held his head as the pleasure continued to build in her.

Suddenly, he lifted her off her feet and carried her to the bed.

"My God, you are beautiful," he said thickly, kissing her lips.

Aching with need, she opened her arms to him as he climbed on the bed with her. "Please come to me now. Hurry. Make love to me. Before we get interrupted."

His laughter washed over her like silk.

"Not tonight, my dearest love."

He slid his body down the bed, running his mouth along each rib, circling her navel with his tongue and moving lower. They'd never had enough time for anything like this. She shivered with anticipation and pleasure.

Doors. Windows. Would Shona be an angel and keep Ella away long enough?

All thoughts of interruption disappeared when Gregory slid his hands beneath her bottom and ran his tongue along the lips of her sex. A molten frenzy erupted within her. She nearly crawled out of her skin at the force of the sensation. As he kept building the relentless intensity with his tongue and his mouth, her mind emptied of all worries and centered on the coming release. Then, when he suckled the core of her pleasure, she shattered, driven beyond the edge of reason, exploding into another starlit dimension, her cries of release echoing around her.

As she floated in that ethereal state, she was only vaguely aware of his body moving over her, his mouth closing over hers.

Suddenly, she needed him, wanted him inside of her. Her fingers moved down over the taut muscles of his stomach and wrapped around the velvety length of his erection. She heard his sharp intake of breath as she guided the smooth head to the opening of her sex.

"Take me, my love," she pleaded, again fearing the imminent knock at the door.

He entered her, slowly at first and she felt herself stretch to take all of him in.

Like the other times they'd made love, she expected him to hurry, but tonight he took his time. Feeling him fully embedded in her body, she sighed with pleasure and wrapped herself around him as he began to move. Long, deliberate strokes wrought a different thrill within her, driving her higher as she looked into his eyes and felt his skin go damp beneath the touch of her fingers.

The door, the window, and the interruptions meant

nothing now. Her body rose with each stroke, and her mind emptied of everything but the man she loved.

He reached between their bodies and touched her, and she came once again. This time her release went on and on until his name became a muffled chant against his shoulder.

In the next moment, he gripped her hips and, muscles clenching, he whispered her name as he poured himself into her.

Freya marveled at his beauty, at his strength, and at the sound of her name on his lips. Finally spent, he collapsed on top of her, his head dropping to the curve of her throat.

They both tried to catch their breath. Their bodies were still joined. The warm feeling of happiness and contentment washed through her. There was nowhere else in the world that she wished to be. There was nothing else that she wanted but this happiness of a life with him.

She glanced at the still quiet door and smiled. With him and with Ella.

"What did you blackmail her with?" she asked with a contented sigh.

"With a baby."

He lifted his head and looked down at her.

"She wants a baby brother or sister. I simply told her we have to dance all night...with no interruptions."

She smiled and raised her lips to his. "My brilliant husband."

EPILOGUE

Christmas Eve

BARONSFORD LOOMED above the frozen lake, stately and majestic, its windows lit with candles. Blazing torches illuminated paths leading from the house to the ice, with branches going off into the magnificent gardens.

The Pennington family and their tenants, neighbors, and guests had gathered for their traditional celebrations, and the annual Christmas Eve skating party was now going strong. The entire household—from the aging earl and countess to the very last stable boy and scullery maid—was partaking in the festivities that extended into the Christmas dinner tomorrow and the great ball the day after.

Freya's skates cut into the ice and she stopped. Her eyes were drawn to the carolers singing by the roaring bonfire at the edge of the lake, where wassail was being ladled out into great bowls and passed around. Happy faces flushed with the cold and drink reflected the bright flames.

All of this resembled some joyous dream. They'd arrived at Baronsford two days ago and Freya had been overjoyed and brought to tears by the reception the family had given her and Ella. They already knew she and Gregory had married. He'd written to his parents and siblings from Dundee at the same time she'd written to her father.

She had no worries about her father's reaction. Baron Sutherland was as certain of her judgment as he was certain the sun would rise in the east. Still, her relief was unbounded at the knowledge that Gregory's family also celebrated their union. Freya had no doubt that her father would be packing his trunk to come south for the church wedding within minutes of reading her letter.

Yesterday, Lady Dacre had also arrived. With Gregory and the rest of the Pennington family at her side, Freya had met the dowager and introduced Ella to her grandmother with confidence. And the reaction was better than they expected. The frail and aging lady was delighted. Her concerns about the child's well-being had been answered.

Freya breathed in the bracing night air and gazed at the tall, handsome skater approaching. His eyes sparkled as he smiled and slipped his arm around her.

"Cold?" Gregory asked.

"Not a bit." She snuggled against him.

"Happy?"

"Very."

Around the lake, a score of smaller fires had been lit, and skaters glided in pairs and groups between them. Young ones raced, laughing as they bumped into elders and each other. In the center of all those activities, she saw Ella taking center stage amongst Gregory's sisters as the young women laughed over the child's stories and antics.

"We won't be able to live with her after all this attention," she told him.

"We shall seriously have great difficulty taking her back with us to Torrishbrae," he warned with a smile. "My mother is in love with her, and so are my sisters. My sister-in-law, Grace, believes that Ella is the funniest and most loving child she's met in her life."

"I may need to give her a lecture about what children are really like. You and I both know Ella is a wild wee elf covered in a lass's clothing."

They both smiled as their gazes were attracted to the pregnant Grace coming down the hill supported by Viscount Greysteil, her husband. Their story was a fascinating one, Freya thought, for it was just this past May that the young woman had arrived at Baronsford, half dead in a crate intended for his lordship.

"Let's go over," Gregory suggested.

Together, they skated over to where the elders of the family were gathered by a fire at the edge of the ice. Lady Dacre sat beside Lady Aytoun on a bench.

Ella appeared as well, dancing around them like a sprite on skates.

"Millicent, I can't tell you what peace of mind it gives me to see these two together," Lady Dacre said.

"We're all exceedingly happy," Gregory's mother said, beaming at them.

As Grace and the viscount joined them, Lady Dacre addressed them. "And I must thank you, Greysteil, for asking your brother to escort these two ladies to the

Borders. I'm so grateful to you for bringing them together."

"But it wasn't his lordship's doing at all," a small voice exclaimed.

Everyone's eyes turned to Ella, standing in the center of the group and looking around to make sure she had everyone's attention.

"I'm the one who arranged their bloody marriage!"

THANK you for reading *Sweet Home Highland Christmas*. If you enjoyed it, please leave a review online.

And be sure to check out It Happened in the Highlands, the next full-length novel in this series. Enjoy this tale of a jilted bride, a duel at dawn, a long-hidden secret ... and a second chance at love.

Lady Jo Pennington was jilted by her fiancé once rumors spread about her questionable origins. Her adoptive parents have always provided her with the love and protection she needed to feel secure. Over the last sixteen years, she's molded herself to meet the expectations of others. When she receives a package from the Highlands containing sketches where the woman depicted looks eerily familiar, Jo believes she might have found a clue to the identity of her birth mother.

When Captain Wynne Melfort ended his engagement to Jo Pennington sixteen years ago, he never imagined he would see her again. But after he uncovers information that could reveal the truth about Jo's parentage, Wynne feels bound by duty to right an old wrong and inform her of his find. He didn't expect long-buried feelings to resurface.

As they strive to unravel the mystery of her birth, Jo

must learn how to trust the man who'd once rejected her, and Wynne must reconcile his head with his heart. But as secrets of the past begin to surface, evil forces will stop at nothing to keep Jo from uncovering the truth and reclaiming her legacy. Together, Jo and Wynne must fight the deadly menace lurking deep in the Highland mists.

AUTHOR'S NOTE

We hope you enjoyed the story of Gregory and Freya, another tale in our ongoing Pennington family saga. For those of you who have read our previous work, you're familiar with Millicent and Lyon, the Earl of Aytoun, from *Borrowed Dreams*, as well as Grace and Hugh from *Romancing the Scot*.

Sweet Home Highland Christmas is one of ten novels and novellas that comprise the multi-generational Pennington Family series.

If you're interested, here is the complete list:

— The Promise (*USA Today* Bestseller) - Running for her life on a desperate journey to America, Rebecca Neville promises the dying wife of the Earl of Stanmore to raise and care for her newborn son, James. Ten years later, the Earl of Stanmore learns of the boy. He sends to the colonies for his young heir so he can raise him as a peer of the realm. With no intention of forsaking her vow,

Rebecca returns to England with James to face a future without her beloved charge, but she must also face her tumultuous past.

— The Rebel - Jane Purefoy, daughter of an English magistrate, takes on the guise of the notorious Irish rebel, Egan, and leads a secret band of revolutionaries against the brutality of the colonial troops. Sir Nicholas Spencer is on his way to Ireland to court Jane's younger sister. When he runs afoul of Egan, Sir Nicholas unmasks the legendary rebel, only to uncover Jane. Bewitched by her, he decides to keep her secret and embarks on a risky plan of seduction that will throw her family into chaos, a country into rebellion, and his heart into the throes of a love that can never be.

— Borrowed Dreams (RT *Award for Best British-Set Historical*) - Driven to undo the evil wrought by her dead husband and facing financial ruin, Millicent Wentworth must enter into a marriage of convenience with the notorious 'Lord of Scandal' Lyon Pennington, the Earl of Aytoun. Lyon is a man devastated by a tragic accident that killed his first wife and left him gravely wounded. Filled with despair, he reluctantly allows himself to be lured into the unwanted marriage. A fresh twist on Beauty and the Beast.

— Captured Dreams - Portia Edwards will go to any length to find the family she's never known. And when she meets merchant Pierce Pennington —the estranged younger brother of Lyon Pennington—Portia has the perfect chance to ask for his help. But her stubborn pride keeps her silent. That is, until she recognizes her strong attraction to the brave man who, by night, is known as the infamous Captain MacHeath, smuggling arms by sea under the pall of darkness, all in the name of liberty...

— Dreams of Destiny - Wounded by scandal and the unsolved murder of his sister-in-law, David Pennington is outwardly insolent and arrogant. But nothing will stop him from escorting his childhood friend, Gwyneth Douglas, to Scotland to save the Scottish heiress from fortune hunters. But with their arrival in Scotland comes terrible danger. Now, if they ever hope to satisfy long-hidden desires, they will need to thwart the evil that threatens to destroy both their lives...

— Romancing the Scot - Hugh Pennington, a hero of the Napoleonic wars, is now a grieving widower with a death wish. When he receives an expected crate from the continent, he is shocked to find a nearly dead woman inside. Her identity is unknown, and the handful of American coins and the precious diamond sewn into her dress only deepen the mystery. Grace Ware is an enemy of the English Crown. Trying to escape from her father's murderers, she never anticipated bad luck depositing her at the home of an aristocrat in the Scottish Borders. As she strives to keep her identity a secret, a duel of wits quickly turns to passion and romance...until danger comes to the very doors of Baronsford, threatening to tear the two lovers apart or destroy them both.

— Sweet Home Highland Christmas (*RITA© Award Finalist*) - Freya Sutherland is a desperate aunt trying to keep custody of her precocious young niece, Ella, even if it means marrying for security instead of love. Recently retired Captain Gregory Pennington wants nothing more than to make it home in time for Christmas, but he's asked to escort some travelers from the Highlands to the Borders. His plans do not include a wife and child, and Freya has responsibilities as Ella's guardian. With Ella conspiring to get them together, Penn and Freya might just experience a little Christmas magic.

— It Happened in the Highlands - Lady Josephine Pennington's life was nearly destroyed when rumors spread about her questionable parentage. Years later, when she receives a package from the Highlands containing sketches of a woman who looks eerily similar to herself, Jo believes she might have found a clue to the identity of her birth mother. When Captain Wynne Melfort was forced to end his engagement to Jo Pennington sixteen years ago, he never imagined he would see her again. More than that, he never expected feelings long thought dead to resurface. As they strive to unravel the mystery of her birth, Jo must learn how to trust Wynne. And as secrets of the past begin to surface, evil forces will stop at nothing to keep Jo from uncovering the truth and reclaiming her legacy.

— Sleepless in Scotland - Lady Phoebe Pennington risks her life to expose Edinburgh's corrupt political leaders, even descending into the city's seething netherworld. Then one night, she narrowly escapes death and lands in the arms of the brother of her murdered best friend. Captain

Ian Bell is a tortured man fighting through grief and guilt over the loss of his sister, and he still hunts for her murderer. Fate has thrown them together, but trust is elusive and danger lurks in the dark alleys of the city. For Phoebe is the only one who has seen the face of her friend's killer, and the sinister shadows of evil are closer than she and Ian imagine.

— Dearest Millie - Lady Millie Pennington's future looks bright until fate deals her a tragic hand in the form of cancer. Dermot McKendry is a former surgeon in the Royal Navy who has returned to open a hospital in the Highlands. Providence brings them together, but life's calamities will sorely test the healing power of the human heart.

— How to Ditch a Duke - Lady Taylor Fleming is an heiress with a suitor on her tail. Her step-by-step plan to ditch him is simple. But there is nothing simple about the Duke of Bamberg. Taylor tries to escape to the sanctuary of the Highlands, but her plans become complicated when the duke arrives at her door and her loyal allies desert her. And even with the best-laid plans, things can go awry...

Finally, if second-chance romance with a twist interests you, be sure to check out *Jane Austen CANNOT Marry!*

As authors, we love feedback. We write our stories for our readers, and we'd love to hear from you. We are constantly learning, so please help us write stories that you will cherish and recommend to your friends. Please sign up for news and updates and follow us on BookBub.

As always, if you liked *Sweet Home Highland Christmas,* please leave a review online, and don't miss Jo Pennington's story in It Happened in the Highlands.

ABOUT THE AUTHOR

USA Today Bestselling Authors Nikoo and Jim McGoldrick have crafted over fifty fast-paced, conflict-filled novels, along with two works of nonfiction, under the pseudonyms May McGoldrick, Jan Coffey, and Nik James.

These popular and prolific authors write historical romance, suspense, mystery, historical Westerns, and young adult novels. They are four-time Rita Award Finalists and the winners of numerous awards for their writing, including the Daphne DeMaurier Award for Excellence, the *Romantic Times Magazine* Reviewers' Choice Award, three NJRW Golden Leaf Awards, two Holt Medallions, and the Connecticut Press Club Award for Best Fiction. Their work is included in the Popular Culture Library collection of the National Museum of Scotland.

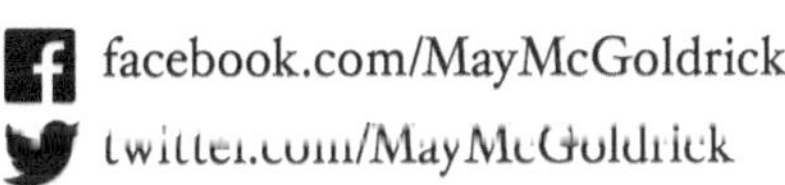

facebook.com/MayMcGoldrick

twitter.com/MayMcGoldrick

instagram.com/maymcgoldrick

bookbub.com/authors/may-mcgoldrick